HELLHOUND ORIGINS

THE RED DRAGON

RUE VOLLEY

HOT INK PRESS

This is a work of fiction. All characters and events portrayed in this novel are fictitious and are products of the author's imagination and any resemblance to actual events, or locales or persons, living or dead are entirely coincidental.

Published by Hot Ink Press

❦ Created with Vellum

QUOTE

No legacy is so rich as honesty.
~William Shakespeare

LOVE

Love.

The worst of all four-letter words.

Nothing trumps it, but loyalty.

Just as treacherous. Just as devastating.

Both have ruled over me for as long as I can remember.

Love.

I stared down at my hands and spotted the slight tremor.

He always does this to me. Always.

My name is Dorin. I'm a vampire. I'm a slayer of the king of all vampires.

Dracula or as I knew him, Vlad the Impaler.

But before I killed him, I loved him.

More than anything. More than salvation.

For that, I traded my soul...

THE RED DRAGON

"**Mercy, dragon!**" the man screamed. I stood above him with my sword raised and eyes burning with the fire of battle. My chest rose and fell in the chilled air. With a sudden jolt, I could feel it in my lungs, bringing me back to life and out of my bloody stupor.

War does this to a man. It will turn you into an animal. Fighting to survive amongst dismembered body parts and deathly moaning. A disgusting display of what we're capable of when forced to choose survival over civility.

My wild eyes remained transfixed on my mortally wounded prey. The man fell to his knees on the ground before me. My compassion fought for him. I tried my best to ignore my weakness.

Mercy. I cannot afford it. I'm not tasked with mercy. I'm tasked with destruction.

The muscles tensed in my arms. Tearing at my will like a rabid dog. My blood coursed through my veins, swelling my heart when it should be shriveling. The weight of my sword felt heavier as my adrenaline faltered. Failing me, when it should drive me forward.

His muddied hands shook in front of me. His eyes were filled with tears. He was discovering his faith. The stark realization was settling into his weary soul. The end was near. I've seen this over and over again on the field of battle.

Men foolishly rushing in with no education to serve as their guide.

I knew exactly what my fate was, and I'd made my peace with it.

I noticed his wedding band, forged of cheap metal on his left hand.

Was he a father? Would his children mourn him? Or was he abusive as mine had been to me? I hated my father and in between his drunken rampages and offensive nature I had become callous when it was needed. My father had made me worthy of war. He had created me, not only in the flesh but stone. He had beaten the *gentle nature* out of me. The same gentle nature that he was desperate to extinguish inside of me. He claimed it would cost me my life. That I could never survive in this world if I found so much beauty in it.

The truth was, he feared me. He didn't understand me. He didn't realize that I enjoyed dolls and dressing up in mother's clothing. He couldn't wrap his mind around it, so he did what he felt he had to do. Ignorant of my true nature and unwilling to accept me as I am.

This sent my honesty into retreat and my life into turmoil.

I hated him and it fueled me with each battle. I drew upon his brutality to do what I had to do for my King. Vlad the Impaler, sovereign King and master of my sword.

My eyes wandered as Vlad slay his twentieth man and let the body drop before him. He paused and let his manly gaze settle on me. My enemy cowered before me with his fingers intertwined and lips quivering. I won't disguise my feelings. It filled me with power. Should I embrace it and with it my true nature? Will it devour me, as fire devours everything in its wake?

Perhaps the word *dragon* is fitting for me. Not that I doubt my King's ability to see through the shroud of deceit. I could never hide from him. I just don't possess the fortitude.

If I have one true weakness in this world, it would be him. He brings me to my knees.

Vlad stood tall on top of the hill, covered in our enemy's blood. His long sword was dripping with our victory. My eyes glossed over as I cried out and it echoed above the battle ground. My sword came down with all of the strength left in me, cutting through bone and muscle with ease. The man grabbed at my sword, now buried deep in his chest. I watched his lips part, blood bubbling up and seeping out onto his weathered skin. I took a short breath and released it. White smoke poured out of my mouth like a dragon. It is what Vlad calls me, and perhaps I am. A dragon of *death*, an instrument of destruction.

A dragon, but loyal and loyalty is the true king.

I jerked my sword upward, and blood spewed out. It shot across my tightly fitted armor and strained facial expression. It reeked of iron. A stench I was growing accustomed to. I quickly turned and raised my sword with honor. Vlad smiled, then he laughed as he held his sword up high and rejoiced in our victory. Our triumph over yet another piece of land he wanted to absorb into his ever growing empire. I cannot blame him for he was orphaned as a child, and I think that his lack of parental guidance ruined him. He was thrust into sovereignty. Robbed of his childhood. Of his innocence. I could see this in his eyes.

Sometimes I wonder if he has a soul and then I remember who I am. I kill just as he does. I have no right to judge anyone or anything.

I'm an assassin, my name known far and wide as a bringer of death.

I raised my sword as high as I could to honor him, my King and a man that I would do anything for. I love him, as a loyal subject loves their Lord and Master, but as I stand here and watch him, my heart fills with something more. An old feeling that I cannot allow to overtake me. It is a sense of want and need for his attention, and I know this is not how it should be. I should be grateful to be in his company and the trusted few who fight at his side.

This feeling first tried to overtake me when Vlad was gracious enough to allow me to stay within the castle walls. My parents were servants of the Dracul family. My father, a blacksmith, my mother, a chamber maid. When plague took them, I was left orphaned. Vlad had taken a liking to me. Probably because our King and Queen, his mother and father, had only produced one heir. His was a lonely life, filled with training and schooling. He was being groomed to rule as he should be.

The library in Castle Bran rivaled all others in the region, and I was

confident that Vlad had read every book available to him. I would have killed to have access to it and with Vlad befriending me, I suddenly did. In fact, I had access to everything. To his library, to his private lessons, to his chamber at night.

His advisors tried to end his friendship with me, but Vlad refused. He fought for me, and that fight stayed with me. It seduced my heart.

He seduced me.

Days turned into weeks, weeks into months and then two years had passed by. Those two years were the happiest of my life. Two years of pure joy as Vlad befriended me and trusted me with his deepest desires.

He wished to one day be King and make me the head of his royal army.

I had laughed at the time, thinking about my true nature. How could I possibly lift a sword, or better yet, take a life?

All I wanted was his attention and love. A love I knew I could never see to fruition.

But one summer day, amongst the cherry blossom trees in the royal garden, Vlad had leaned in and kissed my lips. Gentle, soft. Quick and sweet. I had parted my lips, ready to speak. Ready to profess my undying love for him.

That kiss was my invitation. A welcomed release from my prison.

Just as freedom started to become a reality, we were interrupted by guards with grave news.

We raced back to the castle, only to find that his father had fallen ill, along with his mother, and three weeks later they were both claimed by the plague. The same that had taken my parents away from me.

Vlad was thrust into power, robbing him of his childhood and his fledgling love for me.

The kiss haunted me to this day.

I closed my eyes and could still smell the flowers in the air. The warm sun upon my face. His soft, rosy red lips resting against my own. Then the stench of the battlefield overtook my senses and ate away at my memory, bringing me back to this hellish reality. To the spoils of war.

I lowered my sword as he started to walk toward me. He glanced at my slain victim on the ground, taking very little time to honor the enemy with any of his attention. His eyes quickly locked onto mine. Blue, blue as sky and heaven above. Mine, a chocolate brown. His eyes engulf me every single time. He stopped and placed a hand on my shoulder, and his grip was firm and flooded me with pride. To watch him once again lead us, this small group of Romanian trash, into the battlefield, and always find victory was a miracle that only God had bestowed upon us.

God was who Vlad fought for. His faith was unwavering, and his love for our God complete.

He had blessed us with a warrior and sovereign King.

Worthy of my allegiance. Worthy of my love.

He spoke calmly with a tinge of adoration. "Dorin, my loyal dragon." His hand continued to grip my shoulder. I nodded to him, watching his eyes light up with pride. I know he cares for me as a King should for his loyal guard. The leader of his army. But I hoped in my heart that he could care as he had for me that summer day.

So long ago, so far away. A dream of another life that I could never have.

"My King," I replied, lowering my eyes. He gave me a manly shake.

His voice held steady. "Shed the formality my dear friend, how many battles must we win before you see that I fight at your side as an equal, and not as your ruler?"

My eyes lifted, and I studied his face. He spoke the truth, and it fed my need for him, but I quickly corrected it. "I know my place, if I did not, there would be anarchy."

Vlad smiled. His smile mesmerized me. His lips full, inviting. The laughter escaped him, forcing me to blink. The roar was profound. He is so passionate about everything that he does. It is a contagion, a welcomed virus that is the heartbeat of his people, and for me.

I would know no other life worthy of living if not in his company.

"We ride for home. Then we celebrate, we celebrate as victors once again, my dear friend."

He forcefully pulled me into his embrace. I closed my eyes. He smelled like sweat and blood. His body felt firm against me. It made my heartbeat speed up in my chest. I felt the shame of wanting him in an unnatural way once again. I try to control it, but it becomes harder every single day. My lust disgusts me. My body and mind betray me.

This love that I have for him must die, it must make way for duty. My duty to him is to keep him safe, help him in his conquests and stay at his side.

Vlad's mischievous grin consumed his expression. It was a look not to foreign to me. One that amused, when amusement could be a distant memory at best. We had been fighting for so long. Killing without mercy, expanding this empire.

He winked at me. "You can have as many women as you can fit into your bed, Dorin. Take your pick of mine. I offer that to you. You've more than earned it. This shall be your prize when we return home, victorious. Our people shall be grateful, and the fruits of war shall be ours." I pondered his generosity and the word *ours*. He often referred to our people as *ours*, the victory, *ours*. I wish that it brought peace to my heart when I knew that I should be grateful, too. Thankful that he included me when there was no obligation.

Vlad was the true King. I, his loyal friend and companion. I should not be so selfish and want more.

More would be my ruin.

More kept me up at night.

More had kept women out of my bed and my heart.

He shook me one last time, and I allowed the fake smile to part my lips. I nodded to him.

I lied, as I should. "Thank you, my Lord."

He tapped me one last time and laughed under his breath.

"Now to only convince you that you are welcome to use my name as you did when we were young. Do you remember, Dorin?"

I bit my bottom lip a little too hard. The pain was coming in a distant second to that pain which festers in the dark recesses of my heart. Of course, I remember when we were young. Every blissful second of it. Every night he allowed me to crawl into his bed and stay warm at his side. Every smile, every look he gave to me with those piercing blue eyes. Every time he spoke my name. Whispered into my ear. Let his hand brush up against mine.

And the kiss, the one I longed for yet again.

That was the paradise I stole away to in times of turmoil. A haven where a naïve boy once believed that he could find love within the walls of Castle Bran with its future and now King. Such hopes dashed such dreams folly.

I am but a fool.

"I remember many things, my Lord. Mostly I remember my place and that you are my King."

He shook his head and pulled me closer to him. His breath hot, his eyes filled with fiery passion. My imagination about to run wild. If only the men could fall away, leaving us behind to be alone together once again. Perhaps then he could honestly remember me. Remember how he felt for me, or how I wished he had when we were young. I longed for that more with each passing day. It held me prisoner here. An unwilling participant in a love affair never fully realized.

I cling to fantasy when reality should be my real salvation.

"I suppose I should practice restraint." He laughed. "My bachelor days have come to an end."

I swallowed hard. My throat felt so dry and his words wrapped around it like an iron fist, tightening its icy grip. Choking the hope of renewal from my battered soul.

Vlad had many women in the castle who did his bidding. He was a man who had a reputation for sexual conquest, but over the past months he had slowed down, and one woman had risen above the rest. A woman who I adored and yet envied now. A woman who would bring his bachelor days to an end. Should I be gracious? Should I be thankful that she would bring his conquests in his bed to an end? I wasn't sure if it would be easier to know that he belonged to one, or if I preferred to know that he cared for none that had come and gone.

Regardless, her name was Illona, and she was as kind as she was beautiful. Or so she seemed. She was of royal blood and held herself in a much different way than the concubines who roamed the halls of Bran Castle. My home, or as Vlad would say, *our* home, built in the Carpathian Mountains. She stands as a protection for our people here in Transylvania. A stronghold that had held for generations. A place I felt most secure and yet least loved.

A place that once held my dreams and aspirations.

A lie.

I would never be his. He would never be mine.

Vlad was birthed within her walls, as was I. I, born to servants, Vlad born to royal blood. Yet he treated me as his equal. That was his charm. Making me believe that I was equal in all ways. Stripping away my insecurities and allowing me to be myself. Well, as much as I could afford to allow.

Illona was sent as a goodwill ambassador from a neighboring land. Her father hoped she would woo Vlad and make him take her home-land under his protection. She had been with us for a year now. At first, she appeared shy, homesick, and it eventually drew Vlad in. I can't be certain if she honestly felt uneasy or if it was her goal to attract him to her with her innocent nature.

Regardless, she appears gentle and kind. Unlike any other woman I had ever encountered before. Not that I had bedded any, although I paid a few to spend the night with me to appease Vlad's unwavering need for me to be with them. It seems as if he remembers nothing of our youth. Nothing of me or us.

Vlad spends all of his time now in the cathedral and taking long walks with Illona. Leaving me to watch and prepare for what I know may come…a wedding.

His wedding to *her*. I swallowed hard and accepted it as I have to accept my place in this world. A place at his side, but never *with* him, as I desire.

That seems to be my fate. My Hell. My payment due to our God above.

I collected myself. "Thank you, I appreciate your generosity." He watched my expression with curious fervor. Vlad is not one to miss many things. He was a creature of detailed habit, and it made me nervous each time he studied me.

"You shall find happiness." He whispered to me. "As have I." It seemed like a compromise, a strange admission coming from him.

His words pained me. He sounded so familiar. Just a breath away from allowing his true nature to emerge. But his eyes hardened and the moment slipped away as it always did. He had buried his youth on the battlefield amongst blood and tears. Duty and circumstances beyond his control.

I so wished that I could do the same. My strength fails me in love. I fear this weakness will be my downfall. I feel it all around me, seeping into my dreams at night, confusing me, taunting me.

Do I look like a sinner? A man who would go against God and his will that I lay with women and be grateful to plant my seed? I know I should settle down, or at least consider my legacy, but standing here in this field of the dead and dying holds more weight for me than the thought of living forever.

Here I am. Exactly what he wants me to be, here I get the opportunity to stand at his side. That, to me, is worth more than my name enduring forever. More than a legacy. More than my seed carrying on my name.

My name means nothing next to his.

He saved me yet again by interrupting my thoughts. "Come." He let me go and turned back to the gruesome scene surrounding us. The buzzards circled high above the battlefield. I shielded my eyes from the hazy sun. This was our legacy as we spread out across the known lands, leaving a trail of destruction in our wake.

A warning to all those who would refuse Vlad's rule.

His voice boomed across the battlefield. "Bury the dead, kill the wounded, and then we ride for home." They listen to him without question. Swords rose and fell all over the field as the dying were released to heaven or hell.

The choice made by each of them with how they had lived their lives.

With honor or treachery.

SNAKEBITE

he ride home became treacherous. The weather quickly changed from chilled to freezing cold, two days in. Romanians can endure this, and it solidified our ability to fight in whatever circumstances God bestowed upon us. Our victories rested in *his hands,* as well as Vlad's mastered ability to outwit our adversaries.

Only this was a harsh winter. The most brutal that I had ever remembered. Unforgiving, as is my wicked desire. I could hear coughing behind me. The men were exhausted. Some had injuries that needed to be attended to before they became infectious. This could be a devastating blow to our march toward victory. Rest is a necessary evil. We had been fighting for three years, this time, we had been on this campaign for three weeks. I missed home, as I would assume they all did. Regardless of the ferocity of our campaign, we are still flesh and blood.

Our army is small but fierce in nature. Loyal to a fault. As am I. Ignoring need was something I was used too, but it wouldn't serve to garner success, where success was so desperately needed.

I stared up at our flag as it waved against the gray sky. Stark white with a red dragon engulfing it from corner to corner. It's claws were protruding and fire cascading from its gaping mouth.

I glanced down at the same emblem on my chest. It was beaten and bloodied, but it stood for something more. It gave me a purpose in life. One that I cherished. I needed to focus on this more. The preservation of our people and not my wants and needs. My happiness was nothing next to that. I had given my oath to him, to my homeland, to its people. To fail now would be a tragic reminder of the frailty of men. The weakness of my character.

Something my father would spew at me as he beat me, claiming I was more feminine than manly. Unnatural. He knew me better than I knew myself so I buried that deep inside of me. It wasn't until Vlad entered my life that the old feelings returned to me. Something I could do without.

It weakened me. *He* makes me weak. I can't seem to control it any longer, but I must find a way. I need to pray. I need to ask God for forgiveness and strength.

I held the furs close to me as I gripped the leather strap between my legs. The horse had slowed, and I knew it was hungry and needed rest. I kicked my feet into its thinning sides, and he sped up. I was able to get next to Vlad as he rode with his chin high in the air. Proud as always. His profile so handsome against the bleak backdrop of the countryside. He turned to stare at me. I was shivering, and he laughed and shook his head. It wasn't the cold wind that tore through me. It was him. Always him.

His voice lowered as he spoke to me, careful to keep it between us. "Cold, my brother?" I straightened up and tried to act as if I wasn't.

"I'm all right, my Lord, but the men are tired and hungry...not to mention the horses, we need to rest, or we may face sickness."

"Dorin, please call me Vlad. I think you've earned this right by now, would you not agree?"

We stared at each other for a moment longer than needed. I longed for these private moments with him, yet I hated them. It was a constant reminder of what we felt for one another, even though his feelings for me were wrought with confusion. He could switch from gentle too harsh in the blink of an eye, so I constantly felt at odds.

I took no time to counteract his statement. "I prefer to call you as you deserve, my Lord."

His eyes lowered, and his gaze rested on my lips. "Do you remember when we were young?"

I swallowed hard, and my horse shifted beneath me. It became an extension of my uneasiness.

"Of course."

He sighed, and his breath came out in puffs of white smoke. It escaped his tender lips. I peered at his mouth until I realized that he was watching me. Studying my expression.

"I miss those days. I miss peace." He sounded remorseful.

"My Lord?" I asked, and he laughed and shook his head.

"Dorin, I will break you of this habit. I swear to our God above."

I gave into his request. "Vlad," I murmured as he looked at me. His blue eyes nestled in deep black lashes. So beautiful yet wild, just as he had always been.

"It's nice to hear my name on your lips." He sounded flirtatious.

My breath caught in the back of my throat. His words soothed me, brought me the peace he spoke of. I did remember that peaceful time. A time when we spent our days learning, bonding, sharing our dreams with one another. I longed for those days with bated breath.

I longed for him. I couldn't help myself, as much as I prayed to keep it at bay.

I cleared my throat. "Perhaps we need to suspend this campaign, just for the remainder of the season. Rest."

He tilted his head and stared up at the sky. His eyes scanned the graying clouds and then returned to me. Bright blue and forcing my heart to skip a beat in my armor laden chest.

"I do miss home." He added. "And you." he quickly cleared his throat and turned his horse to face the men. "I mean, the friendship we had outside of battle and blood."

I nodded to him. His words were confusing me even further.

Vlad reached down and touched the deep black hair of his Stallion. He patted it on the side of its neck and talked to it as if it were human. Some men have a relationship with their horses that surpasses that of any human. That is what Vlad felt for his horse, which he called *vânt moarte*, which translates to *Death Wind*. This horse had been with him for years and eventually he will have to set it out to pasture, but for now, it is part of his strength and will. An extension of himself.

Just as I seem to be now.

"Perhaps we should camp for the night and continue on in the morning."

"I do think it would be best for everyone, horses included."

Vlad tapped the side of his horse's neck again and stopped. He turned and called out to the men following behind.

"We rest here. Build shelter, gather wood, and hunt game. Let us eat, rest, and then tomorrow we return home victorious with God's grace upon us." He lifted his fist and shook it high in the air as a few large snowflakes gently glided down upon us. I stared up at the sky and let my breath rise into it. I hadn't eaten for two days, and it was finally catching up with me. I could feel it in my bones.

The murmuring that rose up amongst the men told me that I had made the right decision. I watched him dismount as I caught sight of something in the woods. I jumped down and knocked Vlad to the ground as I had nothing in mind but his protection. I called out to the men.

"Enemy! There!" I cried out.

Arrows flew into the thick woods as I lay on top of Vlad and he stared up at me. I gazed down at him, and his lips looked so inviting. Large and slightly red. My body ached to taste him and yet I knew it would be certain death if I even attempted it. It was torturous to be this close to him. I cleared my throat.

"The thought of battle makes you hard between the legs, Dorin." He said to me as he started to laugh and I rolled off of him. I was mortified that my cock had hardened as I lay on top of him. It was such a disgusting thing for me to allow. I pushed myself up and then reached down to Vlad as he took my hand. I pulled him to his feet. He leaned into my ear, his voice low and his breath hot against my skin.

"I often get hard when the thought of death is upon me. I'm happy to know I am not the only one." He leaned back and winked at me.

I sighed as he walked away from me and a woman was drug back to us, kicking and screaming. She was tossed forward and fell at Vlad's feet as he looked down on her.

He leaned down to study her face. "What is this?" he asked as she looked up at him with hatred. She quickly spat at him. It hit him in the face as I stepped forward and drew my sword and placed it to her throat, but Vlad held his hand up, and I stopped as he wished me to. He reached down and jerked her up to her feet and held her shoulders tightly.

She hissed at him. "You filthy animal."

"Are you alone?" he asked as his voice held steady.

"You killed my family, my brother...my blood. You disgust me." She struggled to break free of his hold on her.

His grip held firm. "So did you come to slay me? One woman, alone?" His eyes scanned the woods behind her and I stepped forward and pointed my sword at the trees.

"Go, search it all. Leave nothing unturned."

Five men ran past me and quickly disappeared into the thick woods. I watched it swallow them whole and then I turned my attention back to her. She reached down and expeditiously produced a knife, raising it high and crying out as she buried it into Vlad's shoulder before I could react. I screamed at her as he stumbled back, shocked that he had been wounded.

I spun on one foot and beheaded her without a second thought. Her head fell to the ground, eyes still open before I dropped my sword and ran to Vlad just as he started to collapse. I rested in the snow, holding him close to me as I called out for help. Our two doctors on the battlefield had now been reduced to one. The master had been slain. The apprentice was all we could rely upon.

I was terrified that he may not be enough for this. I pressed my hand against Vlad's shoulder as he smiled up at me. I could feel his heartbeat in the blood that escaped his wound. It bubbled up between my fingers, hot and sticky. I grit my teeth in horror.

"Always there for me. Always, my dragon." He whispered before he passed out.

I STOOD OUTSIDE **of his large tent**. I heard moaning. *His* moaning. It tore at my heart and every fiber of my being. All I wanted to do was rush to his side and help him. However I possibly could. But my place was standing guard, outside of his tent, making sure that no one entered that shouldn't, and that my protection of him would not waver again.

This is why I hate my feelings toward him. They do make me weak. They ruin me. They force me to focus on the wrong things. I feel as if this is my fault. I was right there, standing so close I could smell the stench coming off of her wretched breath. Yet I had allowed her to wound him. Perhaps fatally. I could never forgive myself for this.

I closed my eyes and lowered my head. Gripping my sword firmly in my right hand and ready to kill at a moment's notice. I needed to push these emotions aside and return to my rightful place. I would never have him, not as I fantasized that I could. I needed to accept this just as I needed to accept that he had a future bride and queen waiting for him at home.

It was my job to return him to her alive, not dead. Widowing her before his lineage could carry on. That would curse me forever.

The loud cry escaped the tent from behind me. Then I heard him call out, but to my surprise, it wasn't for who I expected it to be.

"Dorin! Dorin!" He yelled with desperation in his voice.

I quickly entered the tent and could see him lying there on a pile of soft furs. A makeshift bed for a King. The apprentice attended to his wound with herbs as he struggled to sit up. Another man tried to hold him down, but his strength and will was strong. I sheathed my sword and rushed to his side, staring down at him in horror. His skin was pale, his lips cracking from dehydration. This seemed more than just a flesh wound. He looked as if he may be dying.

I fell to one knee as he reached out and gripped my hand in his.

His eyes pale and glossed over. "Tell her that I love her."

I narrowed my eyes and held his sweaty palm against my own.

"You will tell her this yourself, my Lord."

He shook his head and arched his back. The pain was tearing through him like nothing I had ever seen before. I looked at the apprentice and shook my head.

"Surely you can remedy this."

He looked back at me and his expression spoke volumes before he used the words I did not want to hear. "It appears to be a poison. That demon poisoned the blade."

"What?" I leaned forward and could see the black streaks running from his wound and across his shimmering shoulder. He was burning up. An internal fire was consuming him.

I placed my hand on his forehead and quickly removed it. I pushed the apprentice aside and scooped him up into my arms, rising as he leaned his head against my shoulder. I peered down at him as he started to mumble to himself. I couldn't understand a word that he was saying, but I knew the onset of death all too well. I had watched my mother and father both succumb to this feverish state, and all be damned if I would allow Vlad to suffer the same fate.

DREAMS OF YOU

I **rushed out** of the tent and into the cold snow. My legs ached, and my muscles strained as I carried him in my arms. I fought back my terror and the tears as I reached the edge of the shoreline and blankly gazed into the slowly moving water. I could see the ice chunks floating by in the slurry. I took a deep breath. Calming myself. Focusing on him.

"You will not die this day. I won't allow it."

I walked into the water, crying out in pain. The cold inched its way up my legs, over the base of my back, and finally, I stopped with it resting just beneath my chest. I lowered him into the water. He screamed out to the heavens.

"Illona! My love."

He opened his eyes and glared up at the sky. The snow descended upon us. My teeth chattered, my bones ached. The life force was slowly being stripped away from me. I felt dizzy and just as I started to lose my grip on him two men rushed in and grabbed me by the shoulders. I watched him sink below the surface of the water. The terror of losing him tore through my heart, filling me with fear and hopelessness. He was quickly retrieved and lifted up. He took a deep breath and choked up water from his lungs, along with a small amount of blood. It trickled from his blue lips and over his pale chin. If it weren't for his intense eyes locking onto mine, I would have sworn that death had taken him and me along with it.

I was dragged ashore as he was carried back to his tent. I struggled to break free and pushed myself up to my feet, swaying as I walked toward him. His head fell back, and my heart fell along with him.

"Live! Live!" I called out to him as I fell face first into the snow and lost consciousness.

Dreams of blue sky and flowers floating down from above me consumed my mind. I rolled onto my side and could see Vlad lying next to me. Happy, smiling. Gentle and free. He reached toward me and touched my cheek. I closed my eyes, allowing his touch to consume me. Then I felt the warmth of his lips pressed against mine. It engulfed my senses, and I let the shame and sorrow slip away from me as he took me to a place that I had only dreamed of.

One in which he returned my affection just as I had desperately hoped that he would.

The kissing became harder, needier. I felt his hand lower and press against my abdomen. It excited me and my erection followed without any control. I groaned and rolled onto my back as he climbed on top of me. I grinned at his lips, wanting more. Wanting him to take me.

He gripped me firmly in his hand. I let my lips part, sucking in a much-needed breath. He started to stroke me, forcing me to race toward a climax. His chin rose with each slow pull. My chin was rising along with his. Eyes locked, mouths open. He studied my expression, allowing my pleasure to ebb slowly and flow with each delicate movement of his hand.

He took such great care to preserve the moment.

I twitched, every muscle in my stomach becoming rock hard. He looked down and then back up to me. His mischievous grin teased me. He lowered and before I knew it I could feel the warmth of his mouth engulfing my strength. My power. He pulled back, toying with me. Flicking his tongue and then taking another long stroke with his lips pressed hard against my aching flesh.

His moan rose in the back of his throat. His pace quickened. I felt a slight brush of teeth and hissed uncontrollably. The twinge of pain was only adding to my excitement. He pushed forward, forcing the length of my cock to the back of his throat. He paused, moaning, sending waves of pleasure through my entire body. The vibration was taunting my inevitable eruption. I bit my lip, arched my back, and turned my face. I buried it into the tall, thick grass. I could smell the seasons changing, the renewal of life. He was allowing me to set my soul free. To be reborn into this glorious realization of who I truly am.

His lover, his true soul mate. Now and forever.

A lifetime of his love would never be enough.

I wanted forever. I needed it as desperately as I needed him.

I LET his name escape my lips and reached down, feeling long hair at my fingertips. I opened my eyes and focused in on a youthful girl who peeked up at me from under my fur blankets. I cried out as if I had been stabbed and pushed her off of me. My erection quickly retreated as the horror of the situation sank in. No woman had ever had me, and the thought of it was repulsive.

I shook my head and looked around to see candles lit in a familiar room. We had returned home to Castle Bran.

She sat up in the bed. Her small breasts erect. Pointed nipples aimed at me. I swallowed hard and shook my head.

"I was dreaming."

She grinned at me. "I'm well aware, brave dragon."

I took a slow breath and let it out along with some of the uneasy tension that held my body in suspension. I shook my hands out and looked around the room. I hadn't realized that I left the bed and frantically ran from her. Placing distance between us.

Her eyes lowered, and she bit her lip. "I would be happy to finish if you wish it so."

I bit my lip and grabbed my pants that lay on the ground. I nearly fell over as I scrambled to pull them on, but I quickly regained my composure as I stood up and pushed my shaggy black hair out of my eyes. She rose up onto her knees and stared at me. Her hand lifted and cupped her breast. She toyed with her nipple and sighed.

I cleared my throat. "Food...I need food. Would you mind?"

She narrowed her eyes as her small hand lowered. Her face relaxed, and she grinned at me.

"I only meant to help you. Our King sent me here to warm you up and bring you back to the land of the living."

I stammered and placed my hands on my hips. "I appreciate the effort, now could you, I don't know...perhaps you should get dressed and tell the cooks that I need food. I'm sorry, but my health and strength mean more than pleasure."

She slid from the side of the bed and slipped her white nightgown back on. It was sheer and held nothing back by way of her naked form. I kept my eyes on hers as she stood there in front of me and adjusted her hair. She pulled it back and out of her gown. It flowed red like a lake of blood. The candlelight was capturing the hue in perfect shades as she moved.

"Perhaps you would prefer that I send a boy back with your food, my Lord? Would that please you better than I?"

I paused. Obviously, I had let it be known to her of my true nature. I straightened my shoulders and shifted from one foot to the other. Her words bothered me. I had never been confronted with the truth.

My voice cracked as I spoke. "I don't care if it is you or someone else. I simply require something to eat, nothing more."

She winked at me. "Very well."

Her strange acceptance of me was unnerving. It was the last thing that I needed to ponder. But perhaps it was a blessing in disguise. Her calm attitude helped to ease the tension that had risen inside of me. Something I was accustomed to handling on my own.

She walked to the large wooden door and opened it up, straining as she did so. It must have weighed twice what she did, but she refused to allow it to stop her. She paused and let her long red hair cascade over her shoulder. She spoke with an innocent tone to her voice.

"We welcome you home, Lord Dorin. King's protector and red dragon."

I rubbed the palm of my hand with my thumb and swallowed my

insecurities. There was no need to elaborate on what had just occurred between us. I shifted my thoughts and focused on more important things.

"Our king, he is okay?" I asked, lifting my eyes and staring at her ever so intently. My words true, my intention, sincere. Regardless of anything, Vlad was my only concern. His welfare, my responsibility.

She tilted her head. "Of course, he is, Lord Dorin. You kept your word and returned him to his kingdom." She started to turn, ready to take her leave of me.

I held up my hand. "Wait, what is your name?" I asked.

She turned back and looked me over. "Angela." She said, without hesitation.

"Messenger of God," I whispered.

She took a small step toward me. "What, my Lord?"

I lifted my head. "Your name, it means messenger of God."

She laughed. "Well, I have been called many things, but that is not one of them, my Lord."

"Dorin," I added.

She tilted her head.

I continued, perhaps out of a need to bond with this girl who now knew my secret. "You can call me Dorin. It is my given name."

"My Lord..." she paused. "Dorin." She added. She looked back at me. "Our King will have you seated next to him at this evening's celebration. I just thought you should be aware."

I nodded to her as she smiled and slipped into the faintly lit hallway.

I let out a huge sigh of relief and ran my hand through my bushy black hair. He wanted me at his side at the Kings table. It was an honor to be asked. I paused and stared at my bed. I shook my head and tried to release the memory of seeing her staring up at me as she...the thought of it disgusted me. I couldn't help it.

Then the reality settled into the core of my being. *Vlad had sent her to me. Vlad.* The man that I would die for, the man that I adored and placed above all others. The same man who had kissed me in the garden so long ago.

Tempting me. Forcing my awakening.

Before war.

Before responsibility.

Before Illona.

SHARPEN YOUR KNIFE UPON MY MISTAKES

I sat in my chamber and fussed with my jacket. My hands shook again, and I had to press the center of my palms with my thumbs to calm them down.

I had not been allowed to see Vlad all day. I was informed that he was resting, and it worried me. I had been assured that he was well, but not seeing it for myself left an uneasy feeling in my chest. Something felt wrong, off...amiss. I couldn't place it, but then again, my feelings for him had a way of blinding me to reality.

My vivid dream had proven this fact to be true. I allowed a woman to toy with me. I could not force myself to want them, even though I should try. It just seemed so unnatural to me, foreign. The sin pained me.

I took a deep breath and pushed the memory from my mind. I guess I return to it if needed. It certainly jerked me back into line when it served me best. The thought of her lips wrapped around me, erect and aching...thinking it was *him*. I shuddered.

Perhaps I should remember the beatings that my father had given to me. His hope only to change what I was. What he knew I could never be.

A man who preferred men.

An abomination in the eyes of our God and Savior.

An abomination in the eyes of all we knew or would ever know.

I tugged at my jacket once again with more force. My disgust and anger now guiding me. I despised dressing up, but I was beginning to detest myself more. I just wished that I could see him. Lay eyes on him, confirm his health and well-being. It was torturous to feel this way. I felt lost without direction, lost without a war to give me purpose. Without his hand on my shoulder and reaffirming stance.

A direction governed by the sword and his will. Without a battle, what am I? A sad creature allowing frivolous dreams to consume it. Dreams that will never be. Love that is forbidden and sacrilege. Love that only I have designed.

I tried to shake the uneasy feeling from my bones. Vlad loves celebrations. I could not blame him for that, in fact, I knew it was not the dressing up that had me on edge, but the fact that he had asked that I sit at his side. He had never done so in the years I had been loyal to him. I had been to many a feast of celebration in his honor, but I had always sat across the room, with the other barbarians who fought at his side. His table was reserved for his royal court.

I heard a tap at my door, and I turned as it opened. A guard stood there in his silver armor. A red dragon etched into it on his chest. The red dragon. Vlad's beating heart. He had called me his dragon...*his and his alone,* as I held him in the snow. The vision flustered me until I snapped myself out of it and straightened up.

The guard stepped aside as I nodded to him and she appeared like an angel from heaven. I know that I do not prefer women, but Illona was stunning. She had a beauty beyond anything I had ever seen before, and I knew that if I felt this way, then Vlad must be consumed by her. Her hair was long, black, pieces of it running down her back into a V and resting at the base of it. It lay in long curls, natural. The splintered fragments of daylight played off of it and made her look otherworldly.

Her skin was pale, almost white as snow and her naturally crimson lips rest on her face full and soft. One small indention in her bottom lip, making them even more desirable. Her eyes were large, brown.

Profound and warm. She looked so very youthful, but her eyes told the story of an old soul. Someone that you could easily confide in. Her eyebrows gently arched and her nose was small. Everything about her was appealing. She was built for ruling the masses, from her appearance to the tone of her voice.

Royal, a Queen in waiting. My Queen.

She rushed in and hugged me. I swallowed hard as her sweet smell engulfed my senses. She always smelled of fresh flowers, not too overpowering, but just enough to please. She leaned up and whispered into my ear.

"Thank you for bringing him back to me, Dorin. I worried so. For both of you, as always. I prayed to our God to bring you both home, safe and sound. I should never doubt his love for us, for you, and for our King."

I closed my eyes as her words stung me. I knew I should be grateful that she thought so highly of me, but I was not. Her presence was a constant reminder of what I could never be to Vlad. I could never be *her*.

She leaned back and placed one small hand to my cheek. I lifted my hand and covered hers, reassuringly. I could not deny her the pleasure of seeing me appear grateful for her attention. I gently kissed the inside of her palm as she grinned at me. My lips lingered a bit longer than I meant to and then I heard Vlad's voice behind her. I let her go as she spun around and smiled at him. He eyed me and then his eyes went to her as they always did. Regardless of what he may do to any other woman, she would always have him, his obsession with her was absolute. I straightened my shoulders as she ran to him and hugged him, kissing him on the cheek as he locked his gaze upon me. I took a breath as he hugged her back and then let her go.

"He is to thank for my return. As always, he is my protector, my dragon. I would have died this time without his quick response to my fever, or so I am told. I remember very little if anything at all."

She turned but remained at his side. They both looked at me, and the awkward bit of silence in the room was finally swept away when I decided to speak.

I placed my hand over my heart and spoke with sincerity. "It is my duty to serve you my Lord, you and only you. I am grateful to see you well."

Illona laughed as she tilted her head at me. "Only for him? What about me, Dorin? Am I cast aside as your love for our King clouds your vision?"

My heart rose into my throat. If she only knew how her jesting words had fallen upon truths sword.

Vlad laughed as he stared me down. I cleared my throat and stepped forward. "Of course, I serve you as well, Lady Illona. My loyalty is yours to keep." My eyes went from him to her and back again. I studied his eyes and noticed the dark circles that lay beneath them. His skin was still a bit paler than usual and his lips rosier. I parted my lips. Prepared to ask him if he was feeling better or just putting on airs to appease the masses, and perhaps Illona.

She interrupted me before I could say a word. "Well." She stepped up to me and started to adjust my collar. I kept my eye on him as she straightened it and centered the red dragon medallion in the middle. She let her fingers linger on it for a moment and then spoke to me in a soft tone.

"You are the dragon of Bran, the heart that beats at the center of all things. Kings protector, leader of his army."

I shook my head. "I'm no leader, I follow."

"Dorin."

I looked at Vlad with adoration. He straightened his shoulders and stared me down. He looked as strong as ever, and I felt foolish for doubting his health.

"Did you not question as to why I asked you to sit at my side when we returned home?"

I paused and shook my head. He laughed and looked at Illona, then back to me.

"I trust you with my life. Tonight you take your place as general of this army and my most trusted friend and brother. You will be known as Dorin Dracul, a member of the House of Drăculești.

"My Lord." I choked out as he bestowed a great honor upon me. It was unheard of for the house to take in anyone of peasant blood, but here he was, accepting me as one of his own.

"I guess you are now his favorite, Dorin Dracul," Illona said as she grinned at me. Her eyes wandered from mine to my lips. I felt a bit flush.

Vlad rushed up behind her and picked her up as she yelled out. Her laughter was so full of joy. It engulfed the room. He spun her and then set her down. She tapped him on the chest as she looked up at him. "Behave, my Lord." He nodded to her and kissed her on the cheek. His lips lingered. My eyes locked onto the two of them. They looked perfect for one another. As always.

Perfect and it pained me.

She had brought him nothing but joy. I will not lie and say that I did not feel jealousy. I wanted to bring him that kind of happiness, that kind of peace and tranquility. My train of thought was broken when Illona spoke to me again.

"I am so proud of you, Dorin."

I nodded to her and then looked at Vlad. "I'm grateful for all I have been given here." She stepped toward me. "Well, we are thankful for you. Again, thank you, Dorin. Thank you for bringing him home to me, and to his people, of course."

I watched as they left my chamber and I was bothered by her use of the term 'we'. She had never used that before when it came to referring to her and Vlad. I knew that I should stop torturing myself and be glad that he invited me to sit at his side. I knew that I should take pleasure in our victories and just forget his mouth upon mine. I touched my lips and sighed.

If only I could have him love me as he did her.

If only.

PUT OUT THE FIRE AND MAKE
IT RAIN

*T*sat at the main table, waiting for Vlad to arrive. Illona sat at the other side of his large chair. I reached up and grabbed my drink. Gripping it tightly as my fingers turned white from nervous tension. I took a small sip, and so did she. She glanced over at me and grinned. I nodded as I pulled my cup down, but immediately stood, as did the entire room, when Vlad entered.

He had changed, he had on all red, which always looked incredible on him. His pale skin, black hair and red lips a perfect match for the color. His hair was now neat again. Pushed back, slick against his head. He had shaved the sides shorter since returning home, as he often did. In battle, it often fell into his face. It was something that caused me to harden beneath my armor, this look, the one he had when we were home and civilized, was incredibly mesmerizing. But I preferred the animal. The glossy eyed demon who cried out with his sword raised high. The beast.

That was who I fought for. Who I fantasized would one day take me. Brutal and savage.

My eyes remained locked onto him. He was beautiful in all ways. His face, his jawline, his lips. His eyes always had a shine to them as if he was full of life, and truthfully he was. He was the beating heart of

Romania, the rightful Lord of Bran. His royal blood stretched back to the beginning of time for us. No other had held the throne, but his descendants. He was perfection, a rightful King...to me, and too many others.

Vlad had many a painter sit down and create portraits of him. I always found it amusing because he would sit and then get up, grab the man who was the royal cook of Bran Castle, and have the painter capture his image. Not one enemy knew what Vlad looked like.

He was also brilliant, doing this with his portraits had probably saved his life on the field many a time. The enemy was expecting a man with long hair, a mustache, small build and he was none of that. I am all of 6'2 and he had at least an inch on me. His shoulders were as broad as my own, and his body was sculpted. He was, for lack of a better term, perfection. I was average, although I had been called handsome. My hair was straight and jet black. My eyes large, lips plump.

I watched as he walked the hall, his stride steady and his facial expression that of contentment. I was happy to see him this way, for I had always known him to be restless. Something in him had changed. It was welcoming to see it as he stepped up to the long table and stared at me and then at Illona. I nodded to him and so did she as he made his way up to his large black chair that sat in between the two of us. The throne was constructed of black wood. Spiked and hardened with steel at the two tall points that rose up behind it. Built for a King. Built to intimidate and yet Vlad made it welcoming and noble. We had stayed up many a night when we were young, playing in this hall. Taking turns sitting in that chair, handing out mercy and reprieve.

It intimidated me less than my love for him.

I stood there, shifting from one foot then to the other as my collar irritated my skin. I would be so happy to undo it and be casual later on, but for now, we needed to be prim and proper, just as he wished us to be for this celebration.

He stepped forward and grabbed his cup. He lifted it up into the air, and everyone in the room did the same. He stared at it and then glanced over at me as I joined him and raised my own. He brought it to his lips and took a long drink from it, longer than I expected. I was sure he would make one of his infamous speeches before he took the cup and slammed it down. But he drank it all as the room remained transfixed upon him. He lowered it from his lips and grinned as he snapped his fingers and a boy ran to his cup and filled it again. He nodded to him and then raised it again. The room was silent, waiting for their King and ruler to allow them to partake in the night's festivities.

"Loyal and proud people of Romania, I stand here before you a beaten man."

I narrowed my eyes and glanced out into the crowd as they looked to be as puzzled as I was. He didn't hesitate to go on with his speech, but my confusion lay on my face as it did so many others. Vlad admitting defeat was like watching the sun fall from the sky.

"I have fought for land, I have fought for freedom, but mostly I have fought for something I have always desired. That of legacy, an enduring flame, one that will always shine brightly upon the house of Bran and on Romania as a sovereign nation. I have done this in my father's name, in yours and in the name of Bran to live on in the hearts of every warrior, every kingdom...every heart." He paused and then looked at me. He placed a hand on my shoulder as he continued. "In life we are blessed, it is a blessing from God himself when we find someone who completes us, who we know to be an equal and that you can always trust in, rely upon, and stand beside with pride. I am a lucky man, very lucky." His eyes locked onto mine, and my heartbeat was racing in my chest. His words meant everything to me, and his expression was filled with something I had never received from him before...*one of love.*

I nodded to him and then he grinned and took his hand from my shoulder. "So, here before you tonight I want to say that I have decided to settle down, for I have found one person who is worthy of the legacy of Bran and of whom I want at my side forever." He glanced at me again and then turned to Illona and took her hand. "Will you do me the honor of becoming your husband and King, Illona, as you will become my Queen?" He lowered to his knee as she stood there with a look of pure pleasure on her face. I gripped my cup in my hand and let it tilt at my side. The wine spilling to the floor not so unlike blood as if I had been pierced through and bleeding out to my death.

Death. For that would be the only thing that could nullify this pain and set me free of this torment.

The thunder rang out and echoed in the hall as lightening lit up every window. The fire in my heart, making way for the rain.

I SAT **in the chapel** and stared up at the large brooding cross suspended from the cathedral ceiling. Bright paintings of our Lord and Savior flanked the walls and angels held their swords high overhead, protecting their King, as I did ours. But I was no angelic soldier of fortune. I was cursed, a wretched creature with dark intention, dark desires.

My eyes lowered, and I stared at the symbol of our salvation. The cross was black, black as night and as black as my heart felt after hearing Vlad's words a week prior at the celebration.

I was so foolish to think that it was for me. He never even announced my new place at his table until the moon was starting to fade and the sun was making her way back onto the broad horizon. He had toasted me then, in a hazy wine-fueled stupor. I had nodded and taken leave of his company, no intention of returning, and yet here I sit. A broken man, shackled to him with pathetic memories of what could have been.

I was sinking deeper into a black abyss of which there was no escape. Lingering, when I should be packing my things and moving on.

But I couldn't. I was spellbound, held in place by the mere thought of him.

My love would marry, plant his seed, and carry on as if we never existed. Erasing all traces of me and what I could have been to him in this life. A life I didn't ask for and was now starting to regret ever living.

I suffered from a hatred for Illona, a hatred I could not quell as hard as I tried. I did not want to hate her, she did not deserve it, but I could not help myself. She was, in effect, taking something from me, something I wanted more than anything else in this world. I wanted Vlad to love me as he did her. I wanted his thoughts to be consumed with me.

Then I felt the guilt in my heart. I fell forward onto my knees in the pew. I tightly clasped my hands together and pressed them against my lips. My eyes filled with bitter tears. I closed my eyes, and they streamed down my cheeks as I did everything I could to forget him. To erase how he felt against me. How I yearned for him. His taste, his touch. All of which was being stolen away from me.

I jumped as I felt a hand on my shoulder and looked up to see Illona standing there, like an angel from heaven. The slivers of light in the chapel room lingering behind her head and creating a halo. I sighed and slid back into the pew as she sat down next to me.

"There is no shame in having a passion for him." She whispered as she looked up at the cross. I turned my head and stared at her in horror, wondering how she could have known. Had Angela told her how I raced from my bed, impotent and pathetic? I parted my lips to speak and thankfully she continued, interrupting me.

"God's love is absolute in all things, Dorin Dracul. His passion for us should be matched tenfold. I often find myself in tears when I truly allow his light to enter into my soul." I nodded as I stared at her beautiful profile. Her eyes locked onto the cross and her words full of conviction. She did love God and his blessings he bestowed upon us. I closed my eyes and beat back my lustful thoughts of Vlad. I opened them, and she was staring at me. She placed a hand on my face, and her gentle smile soothed me. As did her touch. She leaned in closer to me.

"You have killed in his name and for the glory of your King. Vlad will always be grateful to you for protecting him and for protecting this land. Your deeds will not go unnoticed. You will always be royalty here, Dorin, regardless of your blood line. Vlad loves you, as do I." She leaned in and closed her eyes. Her lips pressing against my own and I allowed the kiss to linger. It was so bittersweet. The taste of it laced with a slow poison that would surely kill me over time.

Her presence was a poison in my life.

I nodded to her as her lips left my own. She grinned and let her hand rest a while longer on my cheek until we both turned at the sound of Vlad's voice in the cathedral. "Should I be concerned?" he asked as we both stared at him. His words were soon followed by laughter as he walked down the aisle and then he lowered to one knee. He lowered his head and kissed his closed fist. He made the symbol of the cross and then rose up, his eyes locked onto the large black cross hanging there in front of us. He turned to us and nodded, his mischievous grin the only thing calming my nerves. Any other man may have seen this as treason and demanded blood.

Of course, he knew better, but I almost wished that he didn't. Death could find me. I would no longer hide from it. It seems it may be easier than accepting my truth, one that would forever haunt me.

"I would like to go ahead and have the wedding, next week, if you would allow it, Illona."

She stared at him and then jumped up, throwing her arms around his neck and hugging him. A kiss followed, but she quickly stopped when she remembered where she was. I sat there and controlled my temper. I felt the heat rising in me as I wanted to scream out. *"No, don't do this!"* But I would never. I could never say what was in my heart. The darkness that lurked behind my reason for fighting at his side. If I did, then I would have to leave and to leave his side would be worse than death.

I did not enjoy war and killing. I enjoyed protecting him and proving to him how much he meant to me. I knew this now as much as I knew that this wedding would kill me. It would kill off any hopes I would ever have of being with him, convincing him that love does not have to be the way the book says. It just does not. I turned my head and stared at the cross. For the first time in my life I started to feel betrayal. I felt as if God was the one who was betraying me, for as much as I begged and pleaded for him to wipe these thoughts clean, he allowed them to linger. I sighed as I tried to maintain my faith, but honestly, I felt it slipping away with each breath that I took. I cannot say that to be Godless would be a bad thing. In fact, it may offer up a small token of salvation. I blinked as I felt a hand on my shoulder. I looked up at Vlad, who appeared as beautiful as ever, even pale.

"I will need your help, my friend."

I nodded to him as he led Illona from the chapel and I sat there as a traitor to God and all that I had ever believed in.

SECRET ESCAPES

$\mathcal{T}$he metal clashed, and teeth ground together. My footing slid a bit as the young warrior before me tried his best to push me back. He was all of eighteen, a royal, Illona's brother, Stefan, who had arrived for the festivities and the impending wedding.

This union would bind our nations. It was something Vlad knew he had to do but relished the thought of it until Illona had arrived. Once he laid eyes on her, his opinion of it changed. He had complained for weeks prior to it happening, and I had listened to it all, trying to reassure him of how good it would be politically, but now...I wish I had been silent.

Perhaps if I had been he would have second guessed it and canceled it before she even had a chance to come and bewitch him with her charm and beauty.

Bewitch was correct. I had never seen him this way. It seemed so unfair.

I knew he enjoyed her when he rushed our last battle, sacrificing more of his men than he needed to, but he was able to cut it all short by weeks. He had done this for her, and I wondered now if I had fallen there on the battlefield if I would simply be remembered in song by drunken warriors. Would he have mourned me as I would mourn him? I could not be certain now.

I pushed back, and Stefan cried out as he lost his footing and fell onto his back. He scowled at me. He was not gentle like his sister, his eyes were darker, his tone and attitude the opposite of her own. He was being groomed to lead, not follow in any way. It concerned me as I reached down to him and he slapped my hand away and stood up on his own. He was arrogant, and I did not know if he would eventually become a problem for Vlad. If he did, I would be there to stand in between them. A shield, a protector, until the end. I would never allow anything to happen to him, as long as I drew breath into my lungs and could still wield my sword in his honor.

Stefan stood up and looked me over. "You are the warrior, Dorin? The red dragon?" I laughed and switched my sword to the other hand. Giving it one quick toss and catching it with ease. Surely he wasn't mocking me, was he? I had struck down many a man with dirty nails and bloodied scalps. *Men*, not boys.

"Some call me this, most call me death." He grinned as his stance stiffened and I knew he would fall easily. His training for battle had been weak if he had received any at all. I thrust forward as he turned and I hit him in the back. He stumbled forward and onto his knees. His sword slid across the floor and a black booted foot stopped it dead. Stefan looked up as Vlad stood there grinning down at him.

"I see you have met Dorin. He is the greatest warrior in this kingdom."

I placed my hand over my heart. "Outside of you, my Lord," I spoke with sincere conviction.

Stefan pushed himself up and glanced back at me and then at Vlad. "My Father says you have peasants fight at your side, including your dragon. Our guard only consists of royalty, as it should be. You cannot trust the lower class. The breeding is weak, as is the mind." His eyes looked me over with such disdain. Now I understood his bitterness. He was prejudice toward my place in this world. If he only knew that I had earned everything I had received. His lack of knowledge amused me. He may be of royal blood, but his life experience was lacking.

I heard his words and had to laugh. He turned and walked toward me. He lifted a hand and shook his head. "No one laughs at me, peasant."

Stefan stopped dead as Vlad was now behind him. He had one arm around him and his sword to his throat. He swallowed hard, his eyes wide. I would bet he was pissing his pants. Vlad winked at me and then spoke to him in an intimidating tone. One he often used in battle.

"Now listen little one. I will soon be your Uncle, and Dorin, well... seeing that I value him as family, he will be your Uncle, too. So why don't you practice by saying, Hello, my Uncle, I am grateful for your service to King and country. I welcome everything you can teach me, seeing that I know so very little."

Stefan said nothing, so Vlad tightened his grip. He pressed the sword closer to his skin until the boy could feel the cold steel against his throat. He stammered and repeated the words. Vlad smiled at me. He let him go as he stumbled forward and turned to look at Vlad with hatred in his eyes, but he said nothing, knowing better, as he should.

"See...humility is not so hard to find, now is it, Stefan?" Vlad asked. Stefan glared at me and ran from the hall. I laughed as Vlad stood there and shook Stefan's sword in his hand. He turned it and gazed at his reflection in it. He lowered it and peered at me, his expression one of trust and admiration.

"He will hate me, perhaps even wish me dead," Vlad spoke with certainty.

I nodded. "I think we should be weary of him."

Vlad smiled and dropped his sword to the stone floor beneath us. He looked down on the metal and shook his head. "His kingdom is weak, his father likes to appear as if he is a warlord, but he is not. He knows that if he had not sent Illona to bind us, then I would have overtaken him and ruled his lands as I could any other. The only thing I admire about him is his ability to produce a Queen to sit at my side. Someone worthy of Castle Bran and her legacy. With Illona, I will secure this kingdom and its future, forever."

I stepped forward as his words pained me. "Future?"

"Illona is with child. Before we left for battle I laid down with her, and now she will bear me an heir to Bran, a future King. I didn't know if we would return, my friend. The legacy of my bloodline must endure."

I couldn't speak. The thought of it infuriated me. He had said nothing about this, nothing about bedding her for this reason before we left for battle. It now made more sense as to why he wanted to speed up this marriage. This union with her before she would start to show. An early birth could be easily explained, but not if she began to show before he wed her and made her queen. Right now she carried a bastard, after the wedding, she carried an heir to the throne and the future that he dreamed of.

"So is this why you are marrying her?" I asked without thinking of how it sounded. I can't say that I cared. My emotions ruled over me for a split second. He passed me by then turned back and shook his head at me. "I would marry her with or without my child. She is the sun and the moon...the stars for me. I love her, Dorin. I loved her from the moment I laid my eyes on her and to have her is to have everything. Everything I desire."

I watched him turn and leave me there in the cold hall. My armor suddenly felt heavier than it ever had before and my heart shattered into a million pieces.

God had indeed abandoned me, and I made a decision right there to return the favor to him tenfold.

I sat by the fountain in the royal garden and stared at the water and my reflection. A reflection of a man that I no longer recognized. One who had damned his soul as he renounced God and everything that he offered in the so-called hereafter.

There would be no paradise for me. I wished it gone. I had no hopes of entering heaven's gates. Deemed unworthy by the books word. Left damned by my lack of faith.

I reached toward the pool to scatter my image. A rock preceded me and turned my reflection into a distant memory, breaking the surface and shattering it. I turned and stared at Stefan. He had changed out of his armor and was now dressed in a blue shirt and pants to match. His hair slicked back and muddied cheeks washed clean. He was a striking boy who would one day be a handsome man.

"I wanted to apologize." He said without taking his eyes from mine. I could respect this, at least he was willing to admit his wrongs, even if I still knew that he held prejudice in his heart for those not born of royal blood.

I stood up and adjusted my sword at my side. His eyes lowered to it and then he grinned.

"May I?" he asked, taking a step toward me.

I hesitated but then unsheathed it, certain that he posed no real danger to me. He could barely hold his sword, which weighed less than mine.

I placed the hilt of it in his hand and his eyes widened. It lowered until he lifted his other hand and gripped it firmly. He raised it up, and the sun's light skirted across my eyes and made me blink. He laughed as he swung it out and the tip of the blade landed right in front of my face. I grinned at him and peered down the long metal blade. His expression never changed. The smile sat upon his lips and the blade firm in hand.

I reached up and pushed it aside with ease. It lowered as the weight of it tired him. The tip hit the ground, and I stole it back from him. I quickly placed it back in the holster on my side. He shook his head.

"I'm ashamed." He murmured. He walked toward the fountain and sat down on the edge of it. He gently placed his hand on the surface of the water and waved it back and forth. I slowly approached him and took a seat next to him. He glanced over at me, and I at him.

"What has brought you to this conclusion?" I asked. He adjusted himself and faced me.

He leaned in close to my lips and whispered to me. "I prefer men and sometimes women. You would be surprised what secrets they will relieve themselves of while you bury your cock deep inside of them. Angela, especially. Hers is sweet and tight. You should take advantage of this. She is very fond of you, in fact, she cries out your name as pleasure overtakes her."

I swallowed hard and adjusted on the stone beneath me. "Why tell me this?"

"You intrigue me, red dragon."

I bit my lip and straightened my shoulders. "I have no idea what you mean."

He smiled. "Oh come now. Like I care that you cannot remain hard inside of her. I only came here to let you know that you are not alone. I thought that you would find this comforting."

I looked down and then decided to stand up and take my leave of him.

"I have all the friends that I need to confide in."

He stood up and stared at me. He took one step forward. "You could have more. You could have a friend in me. Someone who understands you as you are and not what you try to appear to be. I would even be willing to allow you to call me King if it pleasures you." He reached toward my face.

I cleared my throat. "I will find a suitable replacement to help train you, Stefan."

"Dorin." He called out to me as I left him behind. My heart was pounding in my chest and my skin shining with sweat.

He had now become a liability as had Angela. I wasn't sure how I could correct this without the sword.

SILENT ENEMY

J dreamed of blood and battle that night.

My skin shimmering from sweat and my heartbeat racing inside of my chest. I clutched at my bedding, thrashing my legs. I was in an epic battle, one I felt as if I could not win.

Just as I lifted my blade to stab it into the heart of the enemy below me, he morphed into Illona. I hesitated and then thrust my sword downward, through her chest and cutting into her heart. I felt no shame until the act was done.

I stumbled back as she held a trembling hand toward me, her mouth open, and a small amount of blood trickling from the edge of her full lip. I cried out as I fell to my knees and stared up at the blackened sky. I could see winged angels behind the clouds as the lightning lit up sections of the sky above me. I lowered my head and saw her standing before me. Blood oozing from her chest and my sword in her hand. She walked toward me, and I held my arms out, closing my eyes as she swung the sword to cut my head off...exacting her revenge upon me.

I sat straight up in my bed, crying out as my head detached from my shoulders in the dream. The last of the vision was of her looking down upon me. Vlad stepped up to her side, touching her stomach and then kissed her lips.

My life ending as theirs began.

"MY LORD?"

I turned quickly in my bed to see Illona standing there in her white nightgown. It was translucent, and I could make out her erect nipples. She stepped up and allowed the slivers of moonlight to expose more of her lovely frame. I narrowed my eyes and looked her over. She let it drop to the floor and my eyes took her in. They landed on a small crescent shaped birthmark on her inner thigh. It reminded me of the moon.

"Illona, why are you here? Are you ill?"

She slowly approached the side of my bed and then climbed into it. The look of confusion on my face could not be hidden. She touched my cheek, her hand warm and inviting. Then leaned in, allowing her lips to press against my own. I closed my eyes as she reached under the fur and started to stroke me. I reached down to try to stop her, but she would not. Her grip was firm. I pulled my lips from hers as she lovingly gazed into my eyes.

"I...we cannot do this." She slowed her hand. I hissed, becoming erect in her firm embrace.

"I know what you desire, dragon. I know it isn't what I have. Do you think that your secret will be kept for long?" Then I screamed as I felt the blade slice into me, taking my strength and separating it from my body.

I sat up in my bed and gripped the furs tight. It had only been an extension of my treacherous dream. I tried to catch my breath as a figure walked toward me. It was Angela. She slipped out of her nightgown and stood there with her nipples hard from the chill in the air.

I shook my head as she continued to walk toward my bed then another figure appeared from the shadows. It was Stefan.

I adjusted on the bed and pushed myself backward until I felt the cold frame against my shoulders.

"My Lord," She whispered. "We have come to please you."

I wanted to protest, but my cock stood erect, and I ached with

43

desire. Angela crawled into my bed and slowly pulled the furs off of my body. The candlelight played off of my skin, each curve shimmering with sweat. Stefan stepped up to the side of my bed as Angela reached down and started to stroke me. His eyes lowered and then returned to mine. His expression was soft and inviting.

He crawled up next to me and leaned in. Gently kissing my lips. I moaned as he pushed me down onto my back. He let his hand glide across my chest, stopping only to play with my nipple. I hissed as he twisted it with too much force and bit into my bottom lip.

"Let me pleasure you as you should be." He whispered into my ear. "As only I can."

"Please, stop," I adjusted on the bed and felt Angela's hand moving up and down my rigid shaft. Short bursts of pleasure inched their way down my legs and across my abdomen. My flat stomach contracted. Stefan grinned, letting his fingers move across it. I flinched.

"It seems there is something that I possess skill in that the great dragon does not."

He straddled me and placed his firm cock in front of my lips. He reached down and I could feel his hand under my chin. "Take me." He cooed. The temptation was too sweet. My needs had gone unanswered for so very long. I closed my eyes. I could envision Vlad in the garden, a distant memory, brought to life before me. His skin soft, mouth swollen. His nectar begging to race across my lips and down my throat. I let out a growl that began in the belly of the beast and escaped with unbridled passion.

I gave in.

Tired of fighting.

Tired of wanting and never receiving.

I parted my lips and felt his girth fill my mouth to the brim. He fisted the stone wall and pressed forward, shoving it to the back of my throat. I moaned, deep and abiding. My tongue slithered along his shaft, memorizing each valley, every peak. Committing this long sought after conquest to memory. Replacing his presence with Vlad's, without shameful regret. I glanced up and imagined my King's strength before me. It begged for my attention, so I gave it all that I had, without restraint.

I gave it my sword, my allegiance, my loyalty.

I gave it my love.

He moved his hips back and forth, a slow pace, pleasurable, allowing me to savor it. Angela toyed at the tip of my cock, and it twitched in her hand. She ran her tongue the length of me. Making it shine from what little light played havoc in the room. It hardened with each passing moment, aching to explode with years of built up frustration. Her feminine form did not hinder me. I focused only on the task at hand, just as I had in battle. It kept me erect and strong. Willing to accept that a woman's mouth lay upon me.

Sex is not so unlike that of war.

To survive it you must give into the basic instincts that tear at the heart of thee.

Enjoy each long stride, each stroke taken with the tip of your blade.

Pierce flesh, offer relief. Let the fire consume you.

I cried out for a split second before the length of him quieted my tongue with a deep moan.

She crawled on top of me and slid my extended dagger deep inside. Pushing past her folds and settling into her wetness. I reached up and grabbed his hips, helping him thrust forward. I swallowed everything he had to give, resisting the urge to fight her off of me.

She ground her hips against me. Making my cock ache for release. Stefan thrust harder and harder, moaning with each movement. His strength shook against my tongue, begging for his seed to spill out and down my awaiting throat, but he pulled back, a string of shimmering spit connecting my lips to his throbbing heat.

He quickly moved down and pulled her off of me. He lifted my knees and positioned himself between my legs. I nodded to him as he spat on his hand and rubbed his shaft to a glistening sheen. He placed it against my opening, and I ground my teeth, preparing for what was to come.

He reached over and grabbed the back of Angela's head, pushing her mouth down upon my shaft as he shoved himself into me. I cried out and grabbed at the furs, feeling his massive cock fill me up and force me to submit to it. My ass tightened on him, and he growled like an animal. Each time he thrust into me he would shove Angela's swollen lips down and over my hardened cock, filling her mouth up until I could feel the back of her throat teasing the tip of my sensitive head.

He thrust again and again until we all found ourselves shimmering in sweat and moaning like beasts in an orgy of pleasure. He suddenly tossed her aside, jerking her mouth off of me and grabbing my shaft tightly as he ground into me as hard as he could. With each stroke, he pushed his hips forward, again and again, burying himself to the hilt.

"Take it all, all that I have to give, my dragon." He whispered with a raspy tone. "Yes, yes."

I watched through tear-filled eyes as my cock twitched in his firm grip and my seed escaped me. He rotated his hand, capturing it on his palm and stroking me even further, gliding along with such ease… extending my release and bringing me to a second climax. My ass tightened around him with such ferocity. He groaned, deep and pleasurable. His cock shook like thunder inside of me and his seed spilled out, warm and lustful. He dug even deeper, giving it all to me as Angela fingered at herself and cried out on the bed next to us.

I could only choke out one name as my vision blurred.

I could only see my true love before me.

"Vlad." My lips parted and the last bits of pleasure raced away, bringing me back to a bleak reality. His face morphed into Stefan's. Ending the fantasy as quickly as it had begun.

He collapsed upon me, breathing as hard as I was. His girth was receding as he pulled out.

I quickly pushed him away and tried to regain my composure.

"Well…" he started to say. I raised my hand and interrupted him.

"Leave, both of you. Leave my room and do not return."

He sat up and tried to touch me. I didn't hesitate to slap his hand away from me. The look on his face one of pain and rejection. Angela said nothing as she quickly put her nightgown back on and headed for the door.

"Dorin." He started to say. I couldn't look at him. I was filled with shame for what I had allowed to happen. This was against everything in me, but I had succumbed to it like an animal, a beast...nothing more and nothing less.

"Go," I said as my jaw tightened then relaxed.

He left my bed and quickly made his way to my door. I allowed them to both leave without saying a word. I pressed my face into the furs and the tears came, hot and unforgiving.

"What have I done?" I whispered, feeling so lost and alone.

AS HATE GROWS

I watched as **Illona** walked alongside Vlad in the garden. She smiled, looking so young and innocent. She glanced back at me as I stood my post. Stefan stepped up next to me and stared at them too.

"So Uncle, are you happy about their union?"

"Don't call me that," I muttered. He laughed under his breath.

"Why? Does it fluster you as you remember what I can do for you?" He reached toward me. I grabbed his wrist and stopped him from touching me.

"That will never occur again."

He sighed and looked back toward his sister. "You hurt me, Dorin."

I blinked and lowered my head before I glanced at him. I ignored his admission. No one had hurt him. He was a very skilled predator in his own right. "It is not about happiness it is about a binding treaty and peace."

He grinned and lifted an apple to his lips, biting into it and the juice rolled down his chin. He let it drip onto the ground as he chewed. He swallowed and then pointed at them with the apple in hand. His fingers shimmered from the sweet nectar in the sunlight. I felt like we may be standing in the Garden of Eden. He offered it to me and I shook my head, refusing him.

"I want to tell you something about my sister."

I watched as Vlad and Illona stopped and he touched her face. He leaned down and kissed her just as my eyes turned to Stefan. He studied my expression.

"She can have any man she wants."

I nodded to him. "Her beauty is unwavering."

He shook his head. "Not as treacherous as her will."

I paused and turned to him. "It is unkind to speak ill of your family."

He looked me over and took another bite of his apple. He stopped chewing and then laughed at me. "Oh no, don't tell me that she has bewitched you, too. My dear dragon, was it she who had you ready to go in your bed?"

I shook my head, and my expression hardened. "Don't."

He grinned and swallowed his mouthful of fruit. He cleared his throat and crossed his arms over his chest.

"Our Mother died when I was born. I never knew her, but I heard stories. I know *her, her kind*...and Illona is just as she was, manipulating and seeking power. Like all women are. They seduce for power, and she will take Vlad's strength as her own."

"Who told you these things about your sister?" I asked him as he tossed the apple into the grass. I looked down at it as a large black bird swooped in and pecked at it.

"No one has to tell me anything, all I am saying is the next time she tries to crawl into your dreams...kick her out. She is poison. Don't think that it was by mistake."

"I never said...she didn't...wait, what do you mean by that?" Stefan winked at me. His eyes lowered and rested below my belt.

"Not to say that I would blame her. I mean look at you. I can only hope that you will not always refuse me. Temptation is the true King, and my sister, she practices a dark art. Sorcery. Just as mother did."

I felt flush. "Stop, we are never going to speak of that night again, and stop lying about Illona."

I parted my lips, and he reached down and brushed his hand against me. I made a small noise in the back of my throat. He laughed under his breath. He leaned in and whispered into my ear. "For a man of such stature I am stunned at your naivety when it comes to women, but what should I have expected when you prefer something like me? Just let me know when you're ready…again. I will come whenever you call for me."

Stefan smiled as Illona spotted us and waved in our direction. Dark arts? Illona a sorcerous? Surely he lied. He hates women. That much is becoming clear to me now.

I watched Stefan walk toward the two of them. Vlad appeared happy, unlike I had ever seen him.

I heard Vlad's voice and looked at him as he called out to me.

"Come, Dorin. We are taking a swim."

I nodded to him as I stepped forward. Illona wrapped one arm into Vlad's and one into Stefan's. He looked back at me and grinned. I sighed and followed along until we reached the lake flanking the castle. Private to only our King. I had not visited this spot in so long.

I remembered many a summer that we had swam in these waters. Cool and refreshing. When we were young and carefree, before the evil of the world had begun its march upon our souls. Before we had allowed the enemy to storm our gates and infiltrate our beds.

Before Illona and Stefan had bewitched and bewildered us. Making us weak when we appeared so strong. I felt foolish for believing that we were on the verge of greatness, that we could have it all.

Vlad stopped and stared out at the lake. Illona started to undress, and he grinned. He looked back at me and tilted his head. She stepped out of her elegant dress. Her body perfect, young. Tight and firm. Her skin smooth like silk, pale like a porcelain doll. Mesmerizing.

I found it unnerving that she appeared to look just as she had in my dream, even down the crescent moon shaped birthmark on her inner thigh.

No wonder he found her irresistible, even I found her attractive. I tried to ignore her, but it was almost impossible. Stefan stepped into my view and started to undress. I turned and ignored him. Refusing to give into temptation. Vlad began to take his clothing off. He waved to me to come closer and so I complied.

"Come in and enjoy." He said to me as I glanced at Stefan, naked and running into the water. He splashed as he sank under the waterline and then came up laughing. Illona had already swam out a few yards and was stationary. I looked behind him, and she bobbed above the water and let me see her breasts. She covered them with her petite hands and sank beneath the surface. Vlad continued to undress before me. I stared at him and shook my head, trying to ignore his body and how it made me feel.

"My Lord, if we were to be attacked I could not protect you, any of you."

He leaned in as he took his shirt off and exposed his chest, tight and firm, his abs rolling down his stomach and resting into a perfect V above his pant line. I glanced down and then quickly looked around us. Clearing my throat. There were times that he seemed to enjoy tempting me to ravage him. Because, if we were alone, I would find it nearly impossible to keep from leaning forward and kissing his lips. I desperately wanted to taste his forbidden fruit.

I stared into his eyes. They seemed to be growing blacker in color. The blue slowly being swallowed up whole by a menacing shadow. One I could not place nor deny. I noticed the dark circles still rested beneath them, and his skin had refused to return to its olive tint.

"Do you feel well?" I asked. He glanced behind him. Stefan laughed as he splashed water at Illona and she giggled, returning the favor to him.

He placed a hand on my shoulder and then started to untie my leather straps which held a piece of my armor in place. I couldn't fight him as he continued with his mission to get me in the water.

"No one will attack us, I am Vlad the Impaler, you, my fierce dragon. No enemy would dare attack us here... and yes, I feel fine, except for a bit of restless sleep, why do you ask?"

I looked at his lips and then back into his eyes. A piece of my armor fell to the ground and he began work on my other shoulder.

"You look pale, my Lord, and you seem cold to the touch."

He paused and placed a hand to my face. It sent a wintery chill through me. His hand felt even colder against my flush skin.

"It seems I'm more accustomed to winter now, a casualty of war. The poisons embrace." He glanced at the scar on his shoulder and so did I. It looked faded, healing much faster than any other wound ever had.

"You said *lost sleep*, do you dream?"

He let my other shoulder piece fall into the grass at our feet and grinned at me.

"I dream of great conquest and a noble son born unto the house of Bran."

"And of your Lady, our Queen?"

He glanced back at her and then at me. "No, she is never in my dreams, although I would prefer it. She tortures me, so. I can't tell you how much my love grows stronger for her with each passing day. It swells my heart, as her belly grows." He paused and leaned into my face. "She has bewitched me, as I said before, I am a conquered man."

Those words splintered my heart. I fought back my pain. If only he could feel this way for me.

He reached down and started to untie my leather that laced my side together. Then he undid the other side and grabbed the bottom of the metal plate, lifting it over my head. I let him do all of this without protest. There was no need. I enjoyed his attention because since we had returned, I had received so little of it. My heart was starved, as was my soul.

I nodded to him as he started to take his pants off. He slid them down and stood up, his cock too large to ignore, but I tried my best as I cleared my throat. He laughed and tapped me on the shoulder.

"I order you to enjoy this, my brother."

I sighed and set my sword down on the ground. I stood up as Vlad walked away from me and entered the lake. His perfect ass slowly being consumed by the water beneath him. He suddenly sank under the surface and came back up, shaking his head. His shaggy black hair swung out to the sides. He stopped and waved to me.

"Come." He yelled.

I obey my king.

My Lord.

My only true God now that I had abandoned my faith to the one above me.

I stripped as Illona watched me.

Was she an enemy who had infiltrated the walls of Bran Castle, and that of Vlad's heart? I would not allow her to break him. I would not allow Stefan to break me. I would kill before I would see that happen. I walked into the water and dove in, allowing the murky deep to consume me. Knowing that my allegiance to my King may cost me my life.

SERPENTS SPEAK

*T*he days that followed were a blur of organized splendor. The hunters gathered as much game as they could for the upcoming feast. The seamstress and her loyal maidens worked diligently on Illona's wedding dress. The guards stood at their post. We doubled every man on watch to be certain as the entire castle was caught up in one thing...the union that would be.

All the while I suffered. Guilt-laden for allowing Stefan to seduce me. Heartbroken for the loss of Vlad's love. Tortured by a memory of lying with him in the garden, with white flowers gently floating down above us. His eyes trained on me. His attention, mine.

None of it real. None of it would ever find fruition.

I needed to shed this weakness and return to my former state. Dorin, now known as Dorin Dracul, of the house of Bran. A loyal companion, protector, and red dragon of our Lord's army. Death defines me now. A death I suffered at my own hand.

I feel empty, alone.

Faithless.

God is but a memory.

Love but a torturous reminder.

This defined me, not whimsical fantasies. Not hopes of love. Not dreams of being his or him being mine. I would wither away if not for the sight of him, so I linger, as does disease and famine.

As plague did in this house so very long ago.

Stealing what family I knew and thrusting Vlad into this position of power.

Robbing me of him.

Robbing me of love.

Guest after guest arrived, many from distant lands. Royals from weaker kingdoms seeking mercy and acceptance. They came to show their support and adoration for Vlad. Some loved him, and some feared him, but as he always said, he did not care which…only that they knew he was their true King.

With Vlad it was not about the power, it was about loyalty. It was his undying need to rule as he only thought that he could. He was fair, brutal in war, but gentle in his rule. Because of this, the people of Romania truly adored him. They would die before they allowed anything to happen to him. As would I. I had bound myself to him forever.

I adjusted my red armor and turned to see Illona at my open door. I stared at her as she stood there in white. She grinned and stepped in, taking a quick look around my room. She glanced at the bed and touched her stomach. A small bump was starting to show. Our future King.

"You look very handsome." She murmured. I spied her small frame behind me. I turned and stood my ground as she looked me over. Her large brown eyes compassionate, but I sensed deception.

"My brother talks of nothing but you, my dear dragon. It seems you have stolen his heart."

I coughed uncontrollably. She didn't move. The words took me by surprise and stuck in my ribs like sharpened daggers.

"I don't know what…"

She held a hand up and spoke to me in a calm tone. "Your secret is safe with me. I would never deny one happiness. Don't you agree?"

I narrowed my eyes. "Agree, my Lady?"

"With standing in the way of happiness, of course. You do know that Vlad is happy with me, don't you?" she paused, and I felt my mouth becoming dry. This was not what I expected. Her candid nature was shining through. I started to feel a bit foolish for doubting what Stefan had said to me.

"I..." she looked me over and grinned, ignoring my need to answer her.

"I never understood the pageantry of a warrior until I saw you and Vlad for the first time in full armor. You both embody it."

"I appreciate your kind words, but shouldn't you be with your seamstress today? Instead, you visit me. There is no need."

She grinned as she touched her stomach again and then looked up at me. "I wanted to thank you."

I tilted my head. "For what?"

"For not saying anything to him. Your loyalty is your true strength." She paused and let a small grin arch her lips.

"Saying what?" I added.

"My brother told me that he mentioned things about me, to you. I appreciate the fact that you have not shared this information with our King."

"I did not believe him."

She laughed. "Oh, why would you doubt what I am when I know what you are, Dorin?"

"And what would that be?"

She grinned at me and waved a hand at the large mirror behind us. I turned and looked into it as it rippled against all logic and a scene lay out before us. One of privacy and privilege. The day that Vlad and I had spent in the garden. A private memory that belonged to me and no other. I shook my head and stepped toward it, reaching out as Vlad leaned in and kissed my lips. We were so young, so innocent. Full of life...before war had hardened us. My heartbeat caught in my throat, my chest rose and fell, my breath felt haggard.

"What sorcery is this?" I asked. She stepped up beside me and touched my hand. She felt ice cold. The warmth had left her body.

"I will never give him to you, do you understand this, red dragon?" Her words came out like the hissing of a snake. I jumped back from her when I turned to see that she looked pale with blackened eyes. Demonic in nature, the complete opposite of how she appeared in life.

My voice cracked. "Are you a demon?"

She took a slow breath and returned to her former self. Pale skin, soft eyes, pinkish lips, and rosy cheeks. I trembled inside.

Knowing she had bewitched him. Knowing that her dark magic had infiltrated every corner of our beloved home.

"If you love him you will accept this as it is, as I accept you as you are. We all hide away our demons, do we not?"

"I would never do anything to hurt him, and that was a mistake on my part, I apologize my Lady. I was overtaken with lust. I'll pay for my sins forever."

"Are you nervous Dorin? Do I make you uneasy? I shouldn't. I am just as you are. I love him as intensely as you do, but we need to understand each other. I may appear different to you, but which one of us is truly the demon? One who can transform? Or one who lies in wait?"

"I understand you," I muttered in defeat. Something about her presence wouldn't allow me to gather my courage. She stepped up and placed a now warm hand to my face. Her eyes never leaving my own.

"Good, because he needs you. I need you. This new empire needs you."

I felt a cold wind, and she was gone. I closed my eyes as a single tear rolled down my cheek.

THREE DAYS PASSED and I ate nothing. I barely drank. My thoughts consumed with worry. I had gone from loyal dragon to treacherous snake, not without help from the most conniving of all creatures, that of Illona.

Our secret slowly poisoned me.

My lust for him.

Her ability to shift and cast spells.

He was surrounded in treachery.

She had truly infiltrated this world I lived in, and I did not know how I would survive it. How I would stand at Vlad's side and watch as she ruled not only him but me. She now had all of the power. She had him, this kingdom, and a child who would go on to rule. A creature born of her and I wasn't even certain of what she was now. A demon? Retribution? My fate?

Pathetic that I had allowed it to come to this.

This sorcerous was here to devour us whole. A serpent among men. I could feel the weight of it upon my chest and the longer it festered, the more egregious the wound became.

I was finally summoned to him on the day of the wedding. I stepped into his chambers with dark circles under my eyes and fatigue in my heart. I stood there in my red armor and wanted to tell him the truth so very badly, but I could not. I could not hurt him in this way. He turned and smiled at me and then his expression changed while he studied my face. He walked toward me and placed a hand on my shoulder, gazing into my eyes.

"Are you ill my friend?"

I nodded, just to appease him. "I will have the doctor summoned at once."

I shook my head in defiance. "I am fine. It is nothing that will not pass. I apologize for my appearance, my Lord."

"No need to apologize, my brother. You have not chosen sickness. It seems it is hunting you."

I paused. His words weighed so heavy on my heart. I had chosen this, and it was my fault for allowing her to remain within our walls. I feared what he would think of me if he knew the truth. If he learned of what I had allowed to happen with Stefan. If he was alerted to the fact that his future Queen was a sorcerous. A sorcerous who was pregnant with our future King. And I...I loved him, and Illona knew this. She knew she could destroy me with one wave of her delicate hand.

My eyes lowered as the very thought of it continued to eat me alive. One piece of my now damned soul at a time.

"I wanted to ask a favor of you Dorin, but if you need rest, then by all means, return to your chamber and sleep." My eyes lifted to his own. I could not deny him of anything. "No, I am fine, what do you ask of me?"

He tapped my shoulder a couple of times and then removed his hand. "I would ask that you walk Illona down the aisle for me. I know it is customary that I have my father do this, but seeing that I am alone in this world, I would desire that someone I consider a brother do this for me. Blood or no blood, you have always stood by my side, loyal and unwavering. It would be an honor if you accept my request."

I swallowed hard. I thought about his words and what they meant to him. I knew then as I would always know, that Vlad loved me. I took a slow and steady breath and regained my composure. "Her father will be in attendance my Lord. He should present her to you, not me."

Vlad turned and faced his mirror. He looked stunning. Better than I had ever seen him look before. He had even trimmed his shaggy hair. This I did not expect him to do. He loved it that way and for him to take the time to look less heathen and more respectable meant that he was going into this whole heartedly. He glanced at my reflection in the mirror and grinned.

"I despise him, Dorin, as he despises me. I ate with him last night, along with Illona, and her brother. You should have been there, the pride this man spews. He honestly believes that I am beneath him. That I am lucky to be marrying Illona. It is he who should be grateful. Grateful for our protection. Not that she isn't a great prize because she is."

"Ours," I whispered. Vlad grinned at me and then sighed. He turned and faced me, pulling my head in and resting his forehead against mine. I noticed how cold his skin felt, even colder than it had been by the lake.

"Of course. As I said before, to me, you are a brother...now and forever."

He swayed on his feet, and I placed my hand on his side.

"Are you sick, my Lord?" I asked, and he opened his beautiful eyes and stared into mine. The blue had completely been eaten away by shadow. My heart fluttered in my chest. Even now, I could not control my feelings for him. He grinned at me and moved back only a couple of inches. He stared at my mouth as he spoke to me.

"Her father is a liability. I would ask that you watch him closely. I don't trust him. After the ceremony, I would prefer for him to leave, regardless of what Illona wants."

"Do you fear that they will try to harm you?"

He shook his head and then laughed. "He would be a fool to try, but after this wedding, well…I would prefer if we stay diligent, watchful. Make sure that he is escorted back to his rightful place."

"I would be happy to do this for you."

He smiled. "I will send five of our best with you Dorin. It will be a ten-day ride there and back. Are you certain you can do this, in your state?" he added a small laugh. "You've looked better, my friend."

"I worry more for you. You still lack color, my Lord. It's been this way since you were wounded by that woman. It seems the poison has left you shaken."

He shook me and pulled me in toward him. Our lips so close, his breath hot on my skin. I fought my desire for him. I so desperately wanted to taste his lips. He placed his hands on my face and stared into my eyes.

"Stop worrying about me. Attend to yourself, Dorin. For once. The last thing this kingdom needs is to lose its most valuable weapon. It's greatest asset, our red dragon."

And there it was. The words of truth had escaped his full lips. I am a weapon, as I had always been. I need to hear these words and take them to heart. Bury them deep within my chest and allow them to rekindle my passion. Let my loyalty to this land wipe away my disloyalty to its King.

My king, my lord. My one true love.

I nodded to him. I almost felt as if his mission for me was a blessing. I would be able to get away from everything. I had no way to fight her. She had secured her place at his side leaving me nothing in return. Was I to accept her offering of her brother to me? Visiting well into the night, sucking my cock, as I dreamed of the man standing before me? This could not be my fate.

I STOOD **outside** the large cathedral doors waiting for Illona to arrive. Everyone from far and wide was already crammed into the large hall. All that was left to do was to escort this sorcerous to Vlad and allow her to love him for the rest of his days.

I closed my eyes and clenched my fists as I fought back visions of his naked form in my mind. I still lusted for him, even now. Even with everything that had taken place. I heard footsteps and glanced to my right as Illona approached me, dressed in red from head to toe. Her face was draped in red lace, her wedding dress made of the same. A small string of diamonds rested across her forehead and cascaded down her back. The dress lay off each of her delicate pale shoulders, showing off her protruding collar bones. Her fingers clutched a large bouquet of flowers in red black and white. The colors of Bran, the colors I had always knelt to and honored.

She walked toward me as six maidens flanked her sides. They moved behind her like an obedient flock of birds. She stepped up to me and grinned behind the thin lace. I stared into her eyes as she looked me over.

"You are a proud dragon, and I am honored to have you presenting me to Lord Vlad." I bowed to her as she watched me. The words were absent from my tongue. I had nothing to say to her. She reached down and touched my cheek, causing a humming wave to race along it and down my neck. I instantly felt a little better. Some sort of magic bewitched me. I rose, and her fingers lost contact with my skin.

"I appreciate your obedience, my dragon." She whispered to me.

"I serve Lord Vlad and the house of Bran, including my Lady Illona, soon to be Queen and sovereign mother to our future King." She grinned and touched her stomach. I turned and stood rigid, staring at the two large doors. She laughed quietly and then slid her arm into my own. "Must we always be so formal now, I mean the things we have seen together. Consider me a friend, dear one. Confide in me. I promise to serve you well."

I wanted to fight her, but whatever spell she had placed on me held my emotions at bay and my ability to fight her boiling in my blood.

I clenched my fist. "I serve my King."

"And heir." She said as she touched her stomach. I sighed as the large doors opened and we stood there as everyone in the room turned to look at us. I felt frozen in place until she started to take a step forward and I was forced to follow suit. She walked with pride as did I, passing royal subject after royal. Their eyes raced over the two of us and in all of my days I had never felt so stripped bare. The uncomfortable nature of it stabbed at me as we walked along a path that seemed to take a lifetime.

Illona took her time, slowly taking it all in. She relished it, as I hated every minute of it. I felt like the entire world knew of my treachery now and I could barely look up at the large black cross hanging at the front of the cathedral.

God had truly abandoned me, as I had abandoned him. I had ruined my grace when I spilled my seed into Stefan's hand and his sister's black magic wove itself around Vlad's neck and created an abomination.

A child of this creature that stands beside me.

I almost stumbled, and Illona helped to hold me up. I regained my composure, and we continued until I could finally focus on Vlad, who looked as beautiful as ever.

His expression was one of joy and peace. I had never known him to be at peace before, but it suited him. My heartbeat slowed down the closer we got to him and that of the high priest. I focused on his face. His eyes. Now blackened and foreign to me. The same black that consumed Illona's eyes as she tortured me in my room with memories of him and our forbidden love.

I would fall on my sword if I could only find the strength.

End the suffering, once and for all.

Remove myself from this torturous spell.

Illona whispered something to me and it echoed on the wind. My heartbeat slowed, and all of the worries seemed to slip away. I found peace and tranquility in her voice. She must have known that I was beside myself with guilt and need to confess. She stripped it all away.

We stepped up to the platform, and Illona looked over to me. I turned to her and lifted her lace veil, which was custom. Her lips were exposed first, round and soft, then her small nose, followed by her large and soulful eyes. Regardless of her ability to trick and weave her spells she was stunning, even more so this day. In fact, I had never seen a woman as beautiful as she was. Her beauty radiated in the room, and a small murmur rose up as we turned and I held her hand up. It was also customary for the man presenting the new Queen to her King to show her to the people of the land.

She stared out at the crowd and her grin was genuine.

Her power over us, complete.

They loved her as anyone would. She bewitched those who laid their eyes upon her as she had me. We turned, and Vlad walked down to us. I held her hand out to him and he took it as I let go.

Releasing her. Feeling my heart take leave of me as she stole it by taking him.

DEVIL HIS DUE

*H*er father lingered like a plague in Castle Bran for four weeks after the ceremony. He had claimed he would be returning home, but instead he ate our food, drank our wine, and ravaged as many women as he could have in his bed.

He was a disgusting man, barbaric, but it didn't bother me as it should. Each day Illona would visit me, showing me memories in my mirror, and each day my ability to care waned.

Slowly I was consumed by her spells.

Bewitched, as was Vlad.

As was this entire kingdom.

He rarely spoke to anyone, rarely left his room. At night I could hear him mumbling to himself roaming the halls of Bran. Our world had changed from day to night. Light to darkness.

Illona had cast a deep and disturbing spell over the entire land. Her belly grew, and with it, the creature she had created with Vlad.

Then one night I was summoned to her father's chamber.

"Come, my Lord, please." The guard had said in a desperate huff at my chamber door. His eyes filled with terror and need. I raced along with him through dark corridor and chilled night air.

I arrived to see Illona standing there by her father's bed with a knife in her hand. She turned and dropped it as the blood splattered to the ground. Her face hardened and her eyes filled with tears. I felt pity for her, against all good reason.

She had brought this darkness upon us. This curse to our land. Cast this spell over me which forced me to protect her.

I heard a moaning and spotted Stefan as he started to move on the bed, his naked frame bruised and battered. I ran to him and helped him up, covering him with a white fur. Illona looked on with a blank stare. I glanced down at her naked father, his cock erect and his mouth gaping wide open. She had buried the blade deep in his chest, and the blood pooled around the metal.

"Illona, what have you done?" I whispered in a slight panic.

She looked at me and shook her head, trying to compose herself, but her hands were trembling. I expected her to be stronger, to stand up straight and tell me why she had killed him, but instead she was finding it hard to express her feelings. I looked down at Stefan and shook him.

"What happened here?" He hugged me and sobbed. I turned my face to Illona, who swallowed hard and tears streamed down her cheeks, but she made no noise at all. Her tears were silent. Her voice stolen. She appeared to be in shock. She finally spoke, her voice quiet, as if she was telling a secret long hidden away.

"I heard Stefan cry out, as I had before, only, this time, he called for me. I ran down the hallway and could hear my father yelling at him to stop struggling, and heard the sounds of his fist against skin...Stefan begged for mercy, but with each blow he got quieter and quieter. I could not help myself, I opened the door and watched as father was about too...but I could not let him, I could not. Stephan should not be punished for his desires."

I stood there and held Stefan as my heart sank deep into my chest. She continued.

"My father was a beast, he always has been, but this, he had never done this to Stefan..." she said as she stepped toward us.

"He did this to others?" I asked in horror.

She looked down at her bloodied hands.

"Power is not something you are born with. It is something you acquire. Something you create. Something you take by force." She touched her stomach, and a feeling of dread raced through me. She settled her glossy eyes upon me. "I only needed to become stronger and with this, I have." She placed her hands on her stomach and stretched the material over her skin. I could see movement. My eyes widened in horror.

"What is it?" I asked.

"The future." She whispered to me. "A future where man cannot prey upon the weak. A future where man will pay for his sins."

Stefan kept his face buried in my chest. I held onto him tightly as she stepped up to us and placed a hand on his head. Her voice softened. "Stefan...he was not your father, my brother died in the womb. You were taken from a woman in town. Father refused to allow his legacy to go undone, so he stole you...he took you from your mother and claimed you as his own. I am so sorry. I should have told you. I should have warned you about his perversions. I failed you, and I am so sorry...I truly..." Stefan broke free of me and ran, the bloody fur fell to the ground.

Illona started to chase him, but I stopped her. I glanced at her dead father in the bed. She struggled for a moment, but I held her still until her eyes rose to meet my own. She was so distraught, something I never thought I would see in her. I honestly believed she was nothing more than an opportunist who had taken my home away from me, taken Vlad and everything that I held dear. But, as I held her she sank into my chest and sobbed, releasing her dark past and hidden secrets. Weakened by the truth and sullied by the lies of her past.

I raised my hand and touched her hair. I stroked it, feeling a need to protect growing inside of me. I wasn't sure if it was my sense of duty or the spell she had cast. I felt pity. I realized that she was trying to escape a hell she lived in with her own father. One she had turned to sorcery to escape his evil will.

Desperate, alone. Frightened and beaten down.

She only wanted a better life for her and her brother. Using me, using Vlad...it was her only way to secure her place here. To find a new home, escape his abuse and salvage what she could of a torturous life.

She looked up at me and shook her head. "The child is of royal blood. It is Vlad's heir, but I did not bewitch him to impregnate me, I promise you that. He did this of his own free will. Please forgive me. Please. Please help me, I can't be held accountable for this. They will kill me and along with it, his child. Vlad's legacy. They will also find out about Stefan and you. We are all in grave danger if the truth of his death reaches my homeland. Our guards are as loyal to their King as you are to yours. There will be bloodshed, so many will die." She buried her face in my chest again, and I stood there trying to understand it all and accept her admission and apology.

I RODE **with five guards** with their father's body in the carriage. I would do my duty and return the King to his homeland, but he would not arrive as he had left. I told Illona I would handle this and as I thought about everything I decided that it would be best if we claimed that her father fell ill in Bran Castle and then would die on the way home.

Plague claiming him as it had so many others. It seemed a reasonable explanation. One that could pass as truth. In turn, this would protect Illona, Stefan, and prevent a war. A war we could not afford with a weakened King on the throne in Castle Bran.

I would return this wretched beast to his rightful place without destroying his name, and then I planned to return home with a new resolve and the ability to fix what had been wronged. Illona could be saved. I felt this to be true. Perhaps in saving her, I could also salvage what soul I had left inside of me.

I dreamed of a future, pure and clean. Of a King restored to his former self and a Queen, who could nurture the legacy that grew inside of her belly. A future I now seemed tasked with protecting at all cost.

We rode for five days. Without much rest. I pushed harder than I needed too, but the thought of what lie ahead meant more to me than a good night's sleep. It was reckless of me but seemed logical at the time.

We stopped as the horses needed water and the men needed to rest and eat. I slid from my Stallion's saddle and walked to the carriage. It reeked of flowers and incense. We had packed it to hide the stench of his rotting corpse. His body was starting to turn colors. Not that I pitied him. His soul rested in Hell, where it should. Amongst the demons, damned for eternity.

There was a special place reserved for those who took advantage of the weak, raping, and pillaging. It wouldn't shock me to learn that Illona had suffered the same fate at her father's hands. It would certainly explain her bitterness and need to rise above men.

Death was something I had experienced in the battlefield, but I had never watched as it ravaged a body beyond its limits. Truly, it was a frightening reminder of mortality. I covered my nose as my lead guard stepped up and pointed to the ridge. I could spot shadows and then I could hear the horses as they approached. I looked at him and then back to the men as they rushed toward us at a breaking speed.

I stepped forward as a party of ten rode up and stopped, the man in the middle wearing the colors of Illona's homeland. He stared at the carriage draped in red linen and then back to me. He jumped down and tapped his horse. Glancing at me as he approached us. He stopped and drew his sword, raising it and pointing the broad tip of it at the carriage. The guards behind me clutched at their own as he held a hand up and turned it sideways in his hands. He lowered it to the ground and went to one knee before me. I stared down on him.

"Rise," I said as he stood up and his expression remained emotionless.

"I am Anton, head of the guard of the house of Wallachia, protector to its Lord and heirs." I nodded to him and pulled my sword, I held it sideways and lowered it, rising slowly. "I am Dorin, from the house of Bran. Red Dragon and commander of the army for our Lord, Vlad Dracul."

He nodded to me as a murmur rose behind him. I never formally introduced myself, but I knew that my reputation preceded me as a brute force and highly skilled killer. I had slain so many at Vlad's side that my legend was as secure as his own.

I never pondered this. Not on the battlefield or off of it.

"Lord Dorin, I seek my Lord and Master. He was supposed to return..." I looked at the carriage and back to him, quickly interrupting him. "I regret to inform you that your Lord fell ill and died in Castle Bran. I was heading to your homeland to return your King to his rightful place so that you could give him a proper burial."

"What?" he said as he ran to the carriage and jumped into it. I followed him. He coughed as he smelled the stench of his Lord's body rotting away. He pulled back the red linen and cried out as he saw his face, contorted and sunken in. His cries did not remind me of a loyal guard but more of that of a lover. I had my doubts as to Anton's relationship with his King. He jumped out and shook his head as his eyes looked glossy and his guard watched on in horror.

"What sickness struck him down?" I stared at him, hoping I would sound convincing. "It was fever, a terrible fever that ravaged him for days. I wish that I could tell you that he did not suffer, but I am afraid that I cannot."

Anton stumbled from the carriage and then stopped, he reached down and picked up his sword, steadying himself. I hoped that I had sounded convincing. He held his sword, glancing at me and then slid it into his sheath. I relaxed a little bit as he returned to his horse and climbed up. He gripped the reins tightly in his hands.

"I would ask that you relinquish this task, we can take our Lord home and give him a proper burial. There is no need for you and your men to travel any further."

I stepped forward, ready to argue, but he called out to his guard to surround the carriage, and I stepped back as he rode up to me. He looked down on me and his facial expression remained somber. He was visibly shaken.

"Is Lady Illona and Stefan in good health?"

I nodded to him. "Yes, both are."

"Good, send them my blessings."

I nodded to him as he started to ride off, his guard taking the carriage of their fallen Lord with them. I sighed and looked back at my men.

Suddenly a horse came galloping up alongside him, and their party stopped. He turned back and rode toward us. I stood my ground as he approached me.

He paused and his horse shifted from one foot to the other, antsy and irritated, as was his master.

"Drop your sword, Lord Dorin." He said as he unsheathed his sword and gripped it firmly in his black gloved hand. My eyebrow rose. I started to reach for my sword just as I spotted Stefan riding up to the boy who had spoken to Anton.

He stared at me and then turned, kicking into his horse's sides and riding off toward his homeland. I swallowed hard and tried to make sense of it all.

"I apologize, I don't understand what this is about."

Anton rode up next to me and flipped his sword in his hand, lifting the hilt into the air above me.

"Murder of our King."

His hand came down, the hilt of his sword striking me on the side of the head. Everything faded to black.

PAYMENT DUE

I woke to a stench the likes of which I had never experienced before. Rotting flesh and stinking iron filled the air. I coughed and rolled onto my side, feeling the heavy chains attached to each wrist. I sat up and pressed my back against the moisture laden wall. Very little light poured in from overhead, but I could see a small metal grate above me. I leaned to the side, forced to strain so that I could study what it was, only to find myself quickly yelling out as warm liquid hit my face. Men's laughter followed. I wiped my face and grimaced. It was urine.

I shook my head and quickly turned when the sound of the door unlocking rang out in the small room. I pushed my back against the wall and stood tall, stripped of my colors and armor. I stood in my undergarments, filthy from the cells dirt floor. I was no longer Dorin Dracul, I was now a prisoner and at their mercy.

A guard stepped inside and then a shadow followed. I narrowed my eyes, fighting the absence of light, and then he came into focus. It was Stefan. I rushed toward him, and the guard quickly hit me in the jaw. I fell to the ground with a groan, spitting out blood and dirt. I tried to control my laughter, but it escaped me. The irony amused me as none other had before.

Stefan stood above me and then spoke to the guard.

"Leave us." He said calmly. The guard hesitated. "I said, leave us, now."

He complied without saying a word. I pushed myself up onto my knees, and Stefan looked me over. "Are you okay?"

I laughed and shook my head. I raised my hands and jiggled the chains. "Do I look like I'm fine?" Sarcasm thickly laced my tone. *He couldn't be serious in asking me this, could he?*

"Dorin, this was not my doing. It was hers."

"I looked down and spat again, watching my blood hit the dirt floor.

"By *her*. I would assume you mean Lady Illona?"

He shook his head and knelt down to my level. "You have to believe me. I had no idea what message she sent with me. I assumed it was news of her child and the wedding. Reasons as to why she would not return home to bury her father. I did not know they had brought you here until this night. I was not told of any of this."

I leaned toward him. "Then tell them the truth. Tell them that I saved you."

He stood up and paused, biting into his lip. "That may be difficult."

My brow wrinkled. "How can this be difficult? He tried to rape you. Illona killed him, and I agreed to return his body to his homeland as a favor to her."

"I told you that she was treacherous, I warned you."

"Then why come here if you can't help me?"

He rushed me and placed his hand on my face. He leaned in and kissed me. He tasted of bitterness and pure betrayal. He pulled back and sighed. "I could have loved you," he whispered to me.

He stood up and ran out of my cell. I cried out to him as I watched two guards enter the room. One stepped behind me and held my shoulders as the other bludgeoned me with his fist. Each brutal blow knocked the wind out of me. Each hit harder, each vicious strike leaving me to my memories. Flashes of a garden so long ago. With my King. The one who had stolen my heart and sealed my fate.

72

I WOKE TO LAUGHTER. I was lying on my side in a great hall. The chains dug into my flesh and left my skin caked with blood. My body ached, and my soul cried out for freedom.

I wanted so desperately to turn Illona over to this mob, but my thoughts wrapped themselves around the child that she carried in her womb. What of its fate? Did it deserve death as she did? Could I damn it to eternal fire along with her? Even if I did claim this to be true and tell all, who would believe me?

No one.

I was a Kingslayer. A death bringer.

No one would believe me if I tried to tell them that their beloved Illona was a sorcerous, a caster of spell. Poisoning me with her serpents tongue.

I lowered my head as someone spit on me and was shoved back. The crowd yelled out obscenities at me. If only they would hand me over to the people, then my death would be swift. Why draw it out for all to see?

Anton entered the great hall and made his way toward the throne. He reached it, and I spotted Stefan sitting on the large golden chair. The jeweled crown upon his head. In his sister's absence, the kingdom would be his to rule now. His alone to control and conquer.

I started to rise, and a guard hit me in the back, taking me to one knee. Stefan raised a hand, and the guard stepped back from me. I coughed, and then laughter escaped my lips, I couldn't help myself. I stared up at him with muddied face and busted lip.

"King Stefan," I said. He didn't reply.

"What did she promise you, the world? Power? Is this why you betray those you claim to love and admire?"

I felt another blow to my back, and I cried out. The pain flowed through me like the wind.

"Dorin Dracul, Lord and master of the dragon army, also known as the red dragon."

I bit my lip and stared down at the stone floor beneath me.

"You have been charged with the highest of treason, the murder of our beloved King, my father, and father to this kingdom."

I didn't say a word, so he stood up and pointed his sword at me.

"Do you deny this?" he asked me.

I lifted my head and smiled at him, defiantly spitting in his direction. A guard jerked me to my feet and struck me in the gut, stealing my ability to catch my breath. I fell to my side, and Stefan returned to his throne.

"As reigning and sovereign King I pass down judgment for our people and that of our slain master." He stopped short, and I closed my eyes.

"Death!" he yelled out in the great hall, and the crowd cheered.

I WOKE **up on the floor** of my cell after another brutal beating. I had been kept for months. Rotting away. It had left me broken and awaiting death as a release. I deserved this. It was time to end my suffering and allow the world to go on without me. The great red dragon, reduced to nothing at the hands of a sorcerous and her seductive brother. It would be a fitting end to a pathetic existence.

She had stolen everything from me.

My title.

My power.

My King.

What was left for me, but death and hellfire?

A woman entered and knelt down in front of me. She placed a small bowl to my lips. The water felt refreshing, but I choked on it. My body was on fire. The fever raged through me. One I knew all too well. I must have an infection, and without treatment, it could take me before whatever death march they had planned for me.

A beheading, I would assume, which was custom. I had no idea why they had waited, other than the public beatings that happened weekly to entertain the people of this land. I was now a mockery. A joke. A warning to any that opposed their power.

No one came for me. Not Illona, nor my Lord and King. My friend, or as I had believed him to be. It was as if I never mattered to him and it had broken me. Completely shattered my soul. Without him I was nothing. I had no fight left in me. No reason to live.

I felt the water go down my throat, and it burned. It had a bitter aftertaste. I rolled over and continued to cough. The water churned in my stomach. I cried out and thrashed on the floor. The woman stood up and backed away from me, dropping the bowl and its remaining contents on the stone floor as it bubbled and smoked.

Poison. A welcomed end to a long and torturous existence.

I tried to catch my breath and the room spun. My vision blurred, and I could not speak. I grabbed at my stomach. The cramping so severe. Finally, I felt relief. My skin became colder. My heart slowed in my chest. My limbs relaxed. Death was upon me.

"Hello, dear friend," I whispered. My eyes closed for what should have been the last time.

HE HAS RISEN

*M*y eyes fluttered, my fingers flexed. My legs cramped and then I kicked up my knee only to feel resistance against wood. I reached up and felt it above me. I pushed on it, and a small amount of dirt fell through the crack and into my mouth. I spit it out and the panic started to settle in.

I was buried alive, or so it seemed.

I dug at the wood in a panicked fury, ripping my nails from flesh, ignoring the small tinges of pain that should be worse. Perhaps my adrenaline had kicked in as it had in battle, numbing me to any and all wounds. I couldn't be certain. All I did know is that a death of this nature was not befitting for me. No one deserved this, as evil as they could be.

I continued to fight until the air started to run out. I gasped, slowing as I clawed to break free. I started to lose consciousness and then I heard digging above me. Then a tap to the wood. I called out, desperate to get their attention. Surely it was a mistake. Surely, this couldn't be my introduction to Hell, could it?

Wood was torn away, and I took a deep breath, it hurt my lungs. I coughed again, feeling the wetness on my lips. I reached up and touched it, pulling my fingers back to see blood. I shook my head, and there he stood, Stefan. I pushed myself up and took a swing at him, only to fall upon a mound of dirt. He easily stepped out of my way with his hands raised into the air.

"Dorin, calm down." He said to me. I tried to catch my breath, but my chest hurt. It felt like I had been kicked by a horse and left to die.

I raised my head and stared at him with such confusion. "Calm down?"

"Yes." He took a step toward me. "You are free. I have saved you."

I started to laugh, and it forced me to sit down on the edge of the coffin. My coffin. I glared down at it.

"I was buried right here, left for dead. You left me in that cell for months, beaten and dying."

He shook his head. "I had no choice. She wouldn't let me do anything else."

"She who? Illona?"

Stefan sat down next to me, and I could see that he was visibly shaken.

"You have no idea what she has become."

I coughed again and tapped my chest. "I know what she is. She's a sorcerous."

Stefan turned to face me. "No—she is worse than that. She is undead."

I laughed and then quickly stopped, holding my side. It cramped up and stopped my breath for a quick second. I stood up and tried to walk it off.

"Undead, well if that's your word for demon then okay, we shall call her this."

Stefan stood up and grabbed my hand. I looked down at a small black book. "No, she is undead. Not living. She is Vampire."

I bit my lip and held the book in my hand. "What?"

He started to pace in front of me. I watched him, turning my head from side to side while my muscles ached. I leaned over and coughed, blood trickled from the corner of my mouth. I spat it out and reached in, pulling out a tooth in horror. I held it up to him.

"What is wrong with me?" I yelled. He stopped and looked me over.

He pointed at the book in my hand. "That book holds the secrets to ending her life. It is the only thing between us and total ruin."

I threw it at him, and he held his hands up to shield his face. It dropped to the ground and he quickly picked it up and brushed it off.

He shook the book at me. "I speak the truth. She has been poisoning herself for a long time, little by little, preserving her body. It is the same poison that laced the blade that wounded your King."

I stood up straight and pointed a finger at him. "What did you say?"

"I..." he started to say, and I lunged at him. The entire treacherous plan had become crystal clear. I knocked him to the ground and struck him as hard as I could. He struggled to push me off of him, but not before I hit him twice more. Busting his lip open and bloodying his nose. I rolled off of him as he kicked at me. He caught me in the side, and I cried out, forced to crawl on my knees. The ache in my body was becoming worse by the minute, not better.

I leaned back on my knees while he fingered at his nose. He cried out. "You broke it!"

I pointed at him. "I would do more if I had a blade in my hand."

He stumbled to his feet. "Listen to me. It was her...all her. She sent the poisoned blade to your party. She had your King injured, and she is now lying on that stone slab, in your cathedral, ready to rise again."

I blinked a few times and pushed myself to my feet out of sheer will. I stretched my arms out and my bones cracked. I hissed and rubbed my elbow.

"She's dead?"

"No—haven't you been listening to me? She cannot die."

I took a deep breath and coughed it out along with more blood. "You just said she was lying in the cathedral."

"Yes—yes I did, but she is not dead. She appears dead, but she will wake, as did you."

I swayed on my feet and felt my chest. Suddenly my heartbeat slowed down, I cried out and fell to the ground, writhing in pain. I thrashed about, and Stefan fell to his knees next to me, grabbing hold of my hand. I tried to speak, but words failed me. I felt it shutting down, all of it. Lungs, heart, soul. It slipped away from me and toward a heaven that I would never be a part of. An afterlife that now rejected me. I closed my eyes and ground my teeth, body shuddering and time jumping forward then back again.

I could hear my mother's voice, whispering my name while she held me in her arms.

I could feel the belt against my skin as my father whipped me.

I could smell the heat of battle. Blood and stone. Dust and retribution.

The stench of rotting flesh all around me.

Then my heart took its final lumbering beat. My last memory was that of my Lord, Vlad. Standing before me, smiling in the sunlight. His skin tan with health and vigor. His grip on me firm and reassuring. His eyes were bright with life and hopes of a future.

A future now gone, robbed from him and of me.

I could feel Stefan above me. Speaking to me as if it were an echo on the wind.

"Dorin? Dorin?"

Then I could hear it. Easy as someone speaking my name. A heartbeat, but it wasn't my own. It was faint at first and then pounded in my ears, calling out to me. Its sweet nectar flowing through it, a river of living blood.

Blood. The essence of life.

I let out a demonic cry, releasing the last bits of humanity from my now newly born corpse. An animal now resided where Dorin the red dragon had once lived.

Stefan flinched, and I reached up and grabbed his shirt, pulling him to me. I stared into his eyes, mine now red like fire and brimstone. He trembled, as he should.

"I can hear your heart beating." My eyes lowered and stared at his chest. I could see it glowing with what I desired. My mouth ached and my stomach growled.

Stefan quickly reached into his bag and pulled a fresh kill. A white rabbit. He dangled it in front of my face. I jerked it from his hand and bit into its side, sucking everything I could from the small thing. Once drained, I tossed it aside and stood up. I felt better, stronger. Renewed. My eyes darted from one side of the horizon to the other. I could see so far, feel every living thing around me. The beating hearts caused a reaction in me. I reached up, fingering at my mouth and felt the two elongated teeth. I quickly closed it and shook my head as glared at him.

"What have you done!?" I screamed at him. He held his hands up, and they trembled. I took a step toward him and something peculiar came over me. I felt pity, where none should exist.

Here he was, brother to that which stole all that mattered away from me, and yet I couldn't end him. I couldn't bring myself to tear at his flesh and drain him. He deserved it, yet I couldn't. I closed my mouth and felt my teeth shift, holstering my newly formed weapons.

"Lord, I only did what had to be done. You were dead anyway, and I saved you. I gave you the poison that my sister gave to Vlad and herself. I saved you so that you could save him and the child."

I tilted my head.

"The child."

Stefan stood up. "Yes, remember? Illona is with child. The heir to Bran, the heir Dracul."

I looked up at the sky and stared at the moon, full and red. Blood red. An omen.

"The child should die along with her."

I started to walk toward the two Stallions and Stefan followed me. "Wait, wait!" he yelled out, and I stopped and turned back to look at him.

"The child should not pay for her sins."

I laughed. "The child is the product of her sins, a creature, just as she is, just as Vlad surely is now. It's an abomination. We are an abomination."

"So what is your plan? To ride in and destroy her, the child and your Lord and King?"

I pulled myself onto the back of my horse, and it shifted from foot to foot. Uneasy with me as I was with it.

"Yes."

"And what of you?" he asked me.

"Once I destroy them I will task you with relieving me of this affliction. Now tell me, how do we die?"

Stefan pulled himself onto the back of his horse and clutched the book in his hand. "Sunlight, beheading, or a stake through the heart. One made of blessed wood."

I laughed. "Ironically she lay under her demise."

"My Lord?" Stefan asked me.

"The black cross of Bran blessed by the high priest."

I kicked into the side of my Stallion, and it took off, crying out into the night sky as we sped toward home and salvation.

THE LONG RIDE TO HELL

*W*e returned home to banners flying. I entered the town to vacant streets. The eerie red flags embossed with the dragon flew in the wind. It appeared to have been abandoned and forgotten. Dark and foreboding.

My heart ached for the city that once stood proudly. For a King who allowed her people to sleep with safety and forced her enemies to cower in fear.

My King, now and forever.

The storm had followed us, and the rain had begun. Dark clouds surrounded the castle like an army approaching. But no army came. No one would dare. It reeked of death and destruction. It was no longer the home that I remembered. It was now a lake of blood and fire. Turned foul, utterly lying in ruin.

I pulled on the reins, and my horse spun in a half circle. I spotted the first body then the next. They lined the road leading to the castle gates. Each one impaled upon a large stake. Some still in the throes of death. I drew my sword and relieved each one as I passed them by, severing heads from their rotting bodies. They need not suffer as I had. Death should be swift and kind. My death would linger, just like my love had for him, festering in the filth and decay. Lies and deceit.

I can be merciful. I can demonstrate mercy from a soulless shell. Once proud, but now deconstructed.

I have nothing left to lose, which makes me the most dangerous adversary.

We reached the black gates, and I spotted the bloodstained banner. A fallen crest. A dragon now soaked in blood.

It pained me to see it this way.

It was home, just the same. A place where I had planned my future, one that had now been stripped away from me.

I turned my horse to face my companion in battle. "Understand that here we leave the boy behind and become the man."

Stefan nodded to me. He clutched the small black book to his chest. I glanced at it. "Where did you find this thing?"

"Our high priest. He is a master of fighting the dark arts, or I mean, was. He had died before we left for this place."

"Illona did this?"

He nodded. "I would assume so. Listen, Dorin. I'm..." I stopped him with a wave of my hand.

"No need to apologize to me. Apologize to your maker when you meet him in heaven."

He laughed. "I won't be saved. There is no salvation for me. Not my kind."

I shook my head. "Don't discredit your good deeds. I can't imagine that any God would let you fester in hellfire because you prefer a man in your bed. I think the devil has better souls to devour, like mine."

I rode up to the black gates and called out. No one answered me. My horse turned a few times and I decided to dismount and lower the gate myself. No one remained within the walls with a beating heart. I would have heard them. This also meant that my King lay dead, ready to rise again.

I drew my sword and stared into Stefan's eyes. "I can do this alone, no need for you to see what must be done here."

He followed me as I rode through the gates. I stopped and turned my blade toward him.

"This is not a game."

He stammered when he spoke to me. I felt powerful, and he cowered next to me. "The child isn't responsible for this."

"Why do you plead for its' life? You know it's just as dark as she is. A creature of the night, it will be born into the world and bring destruction along with it."

Just then we both turned as a blood-curdling cry came from the Castle. It was a woman's voice. I raced toward the outer road that wound up the castle's perimeter. I pushed as hard as I could until we reached the top, then I dismounted. Drawing my sword and holding it up. I struck my horse with an open hand on the backside, and it took off, racing away from me. I turned back and rested my steel gaze on what lay out before me. Just beyond the tip of blade stood the black cathedral. The crown jewel of Castle Bran. Again we heard another cry, and we raced toward the two large black doors. I pried them open with little resistance. My new form allowed me to do things I did not think possible. I could feel the strength in my body, unnatural, yet needed for this task at hand.

I stood in the doorway, eyeing the long aisle which lay before us. At the head of it hung the black cross. Beneath it, Illona, on the stone slab. She cried out, and it echoed into the tall ceiling. No angel would come to help her. No God would relieve her of this pain. Only one thing could free her. My cold hard steel to her throat, separating her head from the body, evil from her being.

I started to walk toward her, picking up speed with each animalistic groan that escaped her lips. She was in labor and about to birth something never seen in this world. I could feel it in my bones. It made my cold skin ache and my teeth break through my gums. I spit blood onto the wooden floor, and it sizzled. I didn't allow it to stop me. My new found power was a blessing in this time of need. Only a power that matched her own could halt this sacrilege.

"Illona!" I screamed, and she stopped and turned her head. Hissing at me. I lifted my sword and pointed it at her. Making it clear that my intention was just and her end was near.

"You die this day and that bringer of death along with you."

She let out a deep laugh and then cried out again in terrible pain. I started to run toward her and just as I reached the last pew a sword clashed against my own. Vlad stood before me, with red eyes and blood upon his lips. His skin pale and matching mine. He growled and pushed me back. My feet dug into the wood and caused some of it to splinter under my heel. I found my strength and pushed back against him, almost matching his. I leaned in close, eye to eye.

"Don't do this, my Lord. You know this cannot be."

"You will not harm my child." He yelled. His voice cracked in desperation. He didn't sound like himself at all. She controlled his will now. His strength had been stolen just as Stefan had predicted it would be.

His sword lifted, and it came down hard on mine. I ground my teeth and felt my body pushed toward the ground. I was forced to one knee.

"My Lord!" I pleaded with him, but it was to no avail. He only seemed to be built for one thing. Protection. So ironic, as I was once his protector and closest friend.

"Dorin, the red dragon. Leave this place and never return."

I yelled out, pushing his sword up and off of me. I rolled back and landed on my feet. I gripped my sword with both hands. My teeth now exposed and protruding from my bloodied mouth. He tilted his head at me.

He whispered to me. "Don't make me end your life." He sounded almost like himself. Like the friend that I once served and believed in.

"She can't be. We can't be. We are an abomination, demons, Vlad. Demonic in nature." I yelled. My voice weary and heavily laced with a daunting truth. He lowered his head and for one moment in time I fooled myself into thinking that the end was near. That my words had hit their mark. That he understood that what we are is not as it should be. To live on blood, beyond humanity, beyond death. This couldn't be. It was a curse, not a blessing.

Our curse and it needed to end here. End this night.

He looked up at me and lowered his sword. He walked toward me and let the tip of my blade rest right under his chin. His red eyes settled on mine. So beautiful, even in this deathly state.

"My friend, I have always loved you," he spoke with such grace. The words ripped through me. Gave me pause. Illona screamed and then I heard it, a small cry. New life. A child had been born. An unholy thing. Vlad closed his eyes. The whimpering rolled out like waves, and even I felt a sense of sadness. A sense of responsibility. A need to protect this precious thing that now took its first breath in this godforsaken place.

"A Queen." Illona hissed as she raised the child above her head.

Vlad opened his eyes and growled at me. My moment had passed. He lifted his sword and stabbed me in the side. I stumbled, holding onto it, my eyes narrowing. The shock of his betrayal complete. I screamed and ran my sword through his shoulder. He hissed and placed his hand on the blade. He gripped it with such fierce hatred while blood ran down the side of the blade and dripped onto the floor. I smelled it and my teeth elongated even further. I growled and tried to pull his sword from my flesh.

Then I heard it. The crunch of bone and a blade made its way through the front of his chest. He started to drop to the ground in front of me, and Illona stood behind him, eyes red and wild, blood running down her legs and onto the floor. The child cried out behind her on the stone slab.

"A Queen, he gave me a Queen. He is no longer needed." She hissed with hatred.

My eyes darted to it and back to her. She tilted her head and leaped into the air above me. I rolled to the side and then onto my back. She landed on me, snapping her teeth and scratching at my face. The cuts healed as quickly as she created them with her sharpened nails. It infuriated her. I lifted my foot and kicked her off of me. She flew back and onto the wooden floor. Sliding a few feet, but quickly recovered. I spotted the large black cross hanging high above us.

I scrambled to my feet and rushed toward the child. Stefan ran by the stone slab and scooped up the child into his arms and scurried away. I wanted to pursue him, but Illona grabbed my foot and knocked me to the ground. My forehead hit the wood with a loud crack and left a cut winding from my eyebrow to the top of my hairline. It bled, but as I turned to face her, it closed, healing quickly.

She jumped on top of me and bit into my arm, tearing at my flesh. I screamed. The pain ripped through me. Her poisonous bite felt like fire under my skin. I knocked her off of me, and she spit a chunk of my arm out and onto the floor. She lowered to the ground and crawled to the right when I tried to take a step and then she slithered to the left. She moved like a demon of nightmares. A seductive spider with a deadly stinger.

I spotted Vlad's sword lying on the ground and faked a move to my left, and she followed, then I lunged right and gripped it in my hand, turning over as she fell upon me and the sword quieted her screams. She reached for me, long nailed and bloodied as I held her above me. My blade had impaled her. I grit my teeth and then I saw him. Vlad had pushed himself up and was holding a hand over his bloodied heart. It seeped out over his fingers and dripped onto the floor at his feet.

He made his way to us and grabbed the sword from my hand as I rolled out. I rushed toward the large stone slab and jumped, kicking off of it and reaching toward the sky. I grabbed the bottom of the cross and forced it from its perch. It fell, with me on it, I rolled off as it hit the stone slab and pieces of it splintered off. The loud thunderous roar echoed out in the Cathedral. The cross had fallen, the deed, done.

I ran toward a piece of the blessed cross, grabbing it in my hand as it crackled and hissed. My dead flesh bubbled beneath it. I grit my teeth and Illona broke free of the sword and turned to face me. Suddenly she transformed into the girl she once was. Beautiful and innocent. Bloodied and bruised. She lifted her hand toward me, the tremor in it pulled at what compassion still resided within my blackened heart. I paused.

She grinned. "Dorin, my dragon. Please, please help me." She pleaded with me, but there was only one way that I could set her free, and it ended where it began.

With the spark of life.

She stepped up to me and placed her cold hand on my face. Her temperature now matched my own. I closed my eyes, and she leaned in to kiss me. Just before her lips reached mine, I buried the black wood deep into her chest. Finding her heart and releasing her battered soul to damnation.

She stumbled back from me. She touched it and then let her head fall back. The scream that escaped her lips cracked and blew out every window in the cathedral. Once done she dropped to her side, and her shell started to splinter and crack. Long black lines ran the length of her porcelain skin. Across her lips and racing toward her neck. Then she disintegrated into dust. Black and wretched, never to be light again.

I stumbled back, feeling as if I had watched my own demise. This was my future, let it be quick. Vlad moved and let out a small moan. Sunlight started to break through the horizon. I could see it splintering above us. I looked up, and so did Vlad.

"Let me see one last sunrise, my friend." He muttered.

"It will be the death of us."

"Best a noble death than a cowardly one."

I nodded to him and helped him to his feet. We made our way down the long aisle and toward the open doors. We stumbled out onto the steps as I spotted Stefan riding off with the child in his arms. I took a step toward them, and Vlad stopped me.

"No—let it end here, let this be the last blood shed this day."

I held onto him as he lowered to the stone steps. The sun was climbing behind us, and soon we would be engulfed in its mercy.

Vlad rested on his back and stared up at the sky. He let his eyes move to study my expression.

"I meant what I said to you."

"What is that, my Lord?" I choked out through tear stained eyes.

He laughed and blood bubbled up and escaped his lips. I leaned in and touched his cheek. He placed his hand over mine.

"I have loved you since we met. I apologize for my weakness. I was but a coward to not allow myself to be with you. For that I have regret. I should have shown you love, given you my heart, but in many ways, I did. I was just bound by duty, by the throne. By my name, as cursed as it shall be. I wanted my legacy to be one of honor, and now it will be on the lips of children. The monster, Vlad the Impaler. Blood drinker, killer of his own people. Demon of the night."

I wiped the bloody tears from my cheek, and he grinned at me. He pushed himself up and cupped my face.

"Sweet dragon." His eyes inspected mine and then lowered to my lips. They lingered. The warmth of his love caressing me. Soothing my heart and releasing me of my torment.

"Stay with me, please. Please don't leave me, I love you." I whispered. My lips were trembling, my still heart breaking with each passing moment.

He looked down at the spreading pool of blood on his chest.

My voice shook with desperation. "I can fix this."

He shook his head. "The blade was blessed when I became King." He whispered to me.

He was dying, and there was nothing that I could do but exercise mercy upon him. It broke me, forced me to cry out in such anguish. He gripped the back of my head and drew me to him. Pressing his lips against mine. I tasted the chilled blood on my tongue as he forced it inside my mouth and passionately gave to me what I had longed for all of these years. The kiss could have lasted a lifetime and yet ended too soon. He pulled back and rested his forehead against mine.

"Release me from this death." He whispered. I shielded him, allowing the light to burn my back and blister my skin beneath my clothing. I grit my teeth. My body shook uncontrollably. I locked my eyes onto his. My lips quivered, the pain beyond all measure, but I refused to allow the light to take him away from me.

"I need you, my Lord. Without you I am nothing."

He reached up and gently touched my face, letting his fingers glide across it and onto my lip.

"I will always love you, my dragon. My brother, my love."

He pushed me aside, and the sunlight engulfed him. I screamed as I watched his skin crack and disintegrate before me. His dust slowly rose into the sunlight with small flashes of fiery light. I lay down and accepted my fate. Rolling over onto my back and extending my arms.

Without his love, I was lost.

I parted my lips. "Please forgive me, my Lord, our God in heaven. Please accept me as I am. I ask for your forgiveness."

I closed my eyes and felt the heat. The sun cascaded across my skin, and it started to crack and splinter. The pain something I welcomed, for it meant the end.

A dark shadow fell over me. It blocked out the bright light of freedom. My eyes focused in on black wings. A beautiful face leaned into mine. A man with large eyes, full lips, and smooth skin. He looked angelic, pure. Beautiful and seductive beyond all measure.

"God?" I asked.

The man smiled at me and studied my lips. He reached down and touched them, gently moving his thumb.

"Some call me that, but you can call me Lucifer." He paused. I blinked a couple of times and shook my head.

"No...let me die!" I cried out, and he embraced me in his dark wings.

"Not this day, my dragon. It's a long ride to Hell. Trust me, I know."

My desperate plea reached out to the heavens above and fell upon deaf ears.

IN THE BLINK OF AN EYE, I found myself standing on the edge of an abyss. The stench of sulfur burned my nostrils. I peered below me and could see the lake of fire, thrashing about in great turmoil. A face would appear on the surface of the fiery sea, then a hand, followed by another.

"Dorin."

I turned to see Lucifer standing behind me.

"Why am I not suffering as they are?"

Lucifer retracted his large black wings, tucking them behind him.

Now he appeared more human in nature, although his eyes glowed with evil intent.

"This is your chance at salvation my immortal friend."

I swallowed hard and beat back the feelings of dread. "There is no salvation for a creature such as myself."

He clicked his tongue against his white teeth and quickly grinned at me.

"So tormented. Have you done this your entire life? Denied the possibility of hope?" he asked me.

I sighed. "I deserve none."

Lucifer approached me and placed his fingers under my chin and forced me to meet his fiery gaze.

"You asked to be forgiven as life slipped away from you," he whispered.

"By God," I replied without hesitation.

He chuckled under his breath. "Am I not a suitable replacement? Did I not come to your rescue in your hour of need?"

I scanned my surroundings. "I didn't ask for this. I expected death to claim me as it should...as it..." I stopped. My heart ached at the very thought of him. The memory of my love disintegrating before my eyes.

Lucifer quickly positioned himself behind me. He pressed his warm body against mine. His arms wrapped around me and I tried to move, but couldn't break free.

"Salvation must be earned for a creature such as yourself."

My eyes closed. His hand lowered and pressed against my stomach. Lust quickly followed. I ground my teeth together as my new fangs elongated inside of my mouth. I could taste the blood and it excited me.

"I know that my desire was an abomination in the eyes of our God."

He laughed and nibbled at my ear. I shifted my weight from one foot to the other, and he stopped.

"Foolish boy." He hissed.

He moved in front of me and touched my cheek with the back of his hand.

"Your sexual desires do not dictate your ability to achieve salvation."

My eyes widened. "What?"

He smiled and leaned into my face. He smelled of sweet flowers and a blend of sandalwood.

"The only sin that leads to damnation is the taking of life."

I swallowed hard. "I've taken many."

He stepped back and shook his head. "Oh no, none of that mattered. It was war. All's fair, or so they say." He looked at his fingernails and then back to me. "I'm talking about your own surrender."

I sucked in my breath. "You mean when I begged to be released from this corpse?"

He shrugged his shoulders. "I don't make up the rules, I just enforce them and don't play martyr with me. You asked for death so that you could follow him into oblivion. Nothing more and nothing less."

I let the reality settle in. My eyes lifted.

"So what now?" I asked.

He looked me over. "Now you must make a choice. Stay with me and fight for salvation or jump into the lake of fire."

I closed my eyes, and he whispered into my ear. "Be more, become the dragon. Stay with me and his death will not have been in vain. Save others as you failed to save him. Find love with me."

LOVE.

The worst of all four-letter words.

Nothing trumps it, but loyalty.

Just as treacherous. Just as devastating.

Both have ruled over me for as long as I can remember.

Love.

I stared down at my hands and spotted the slight tremor.

He always does this to me. Always.

My name is Dorin. I'm a vampire. I'm a slayer of the king of all vampires.

Dracula or as I knew him, Vlad the Impaler.

But before I killed him, I loved him.

More than anything. More than salvation.

For that, I traded my soul...

I lifted my head and gazed at my new Lord.

"Yes, I will do this, but not for me...for him,"

Lucifer smiled. "Welcome home, my Hellhound."

ABOUT HELLHOUND

Thank you for taking this journey with me.
*Dorin's story continues as he fights with a team of five as a **Hellhound**. Each*
Hellhound is a fallen warrior who asks for forgiveness upon their death. Each
one collected by Lucifer. He joins a Roman, two Vikings, and one pissed off
girl as they battle the rising tide of Hell.

Please follow Rue Volley on Amazon to keep up with the series.

ABOUT RUE

Rue Volley is the author of The Devil's Gate Trilogy, Hellhound, The Blood & Light Vampire Series, a witch's tale, and various novella's released both independently and within anthologies.

Rue is an award-winning author, graphic artist, and screenwriter.
   She is credited with two films.
   Hellhound (original script, 2014)
   Awakening (contributing screenwriter, 2015)
   IMDb: http://www.imdb.com/name/nm7043310/

Miss. Volley began her writing career in 2008 as she penned her freshman effort, The Blood & Light Vampire Series. She self-published the first novel in 2010 and within six months she was courted and signed by Vamptasy Publishing (UK).

Over the course of the next five years, she released over thirty books establishing herself in the publishing world as a prolific writer. She is best known for dark fantasy and mystery erotica. Bringing her wicked (somewhat dark) sense of humor and perfected ability to create engaging characters to her ever-growing fan base.

Rue has a deep love for comic books and film. She gives credit to amazing artists like Garth Ennis, Alan Moore, Frank Miller, Neil Gaiman, and of course, Stan Lee, for her love of the written word.

Rue enjoys walks by the lake, small town living, and spending time with her family. She loves coffee, chocolate, and believes in love, as twisted as it can be.

Rue is represented by Gladys Gonzales Atwell, Publicist, and Hot Ink Press, Publisher as well as Encompass Ink.
    Website: http://www.ruevolley.com/
    Twitter: https://twitter.com/ruevolley
    FB: https://www.facebook.com/Rue-Volley-146299465525490/?fref=ts

Made in the USA
Monee, IL
10 January 2020